The Prayer Chest

The Prayer Chest

A NOVEL ABOUT RECEIVING
ALL OF LIFE'S RICHES

August Gold AND *Joel Fotinos*

DOUBLEDAY LARGE PRINT HOME LIBRARY EDITION

DOUBLEDAY
*New York   London   Toronto
Sydney   Auckland*

This Large Print Edition, prepared especially for Doubleday Large Print Home Library, contains the complete, unabridged text of the original Publisher's Edition.

PUBLISHED BY DOUBLEDAY

Published in the United States by Doubleday,
an imprint of The Doubleday Broadway Publishing Group,
a division of Random House, Inc., New York, New York.

DOUBLEDAY and the portrayal of an anchor
with a dolphin are registered trademarks
of Random House, Inc.

ISBN-13: 978-0-7394-8862-1

PRINTED IN THE UNITED STATES OF AMERICA

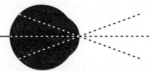

This Large Print Book carries the
Seal of Approval of N.A.V.H.

TO CL
The answer to my prayer

TO AS AND RFS
Proof that prayer works

Easter Day, 1939

🌿 There was a time in his life when Joseph would have bounded up the flight of stairs, taking them two and three at a clip. He might have arrived at the attic door with his children tucked beneath his arms and energy to spare for three more flights. Not tonight, not at seventy-three years of age, the longest-living Hutchinson man.

He climbed the flight of stairs to the attic and stepped into the drafty, dusty little room for what was probably the thousandth time. He took the same uncomfortable seat on the rickety, time-worn, wooden chair and placed the Prayer Chest on his lap as if it were nothing more than a plain wooden box used to store odd coins or objects of no consequence.

But there was nothing plain about this Prayer Chest. For one thing, it was fastened with a tiny lock made of pure gold. For another, this wooden box had saved his life.

Carefully Joseph laid Malachi's ancient notebook atop the chest and flipped it open to count the blank pages. There were two; he would need them both. He dipped the sharpened quill into the bottle of ink he had brought with him and began to write:

This Easter Day, April 9, 1939, written by Joseph Hutchinson

I write this to you, my great-great-granddaughter, Clare Rose. One day, many years hence, you shall read this notebook and ask, "Who was Joseph to add his wisdom to the greater wisdom of Malachi?"

To which I reply: I am a simple man who was almost swallowed up by the sorrows of life were it not for the Prayer Chest you now hold in your hands.

If you asked Joseph the particulars about the year the Prayer Chest entered his life, he might say that 1891 was the year the light of the world went out for good. He might say that it was the year he had gone down into the valley of the shadow of death and feared he would not climb out of it a whole man.

But more than likely he would not say anything, because he would be too over-come with emotion to speak. His eyes would fasten on a distant past, and he would vanish into his memories, leaving you behind to wonder what had happened.

Joseph would be right to say that the Prayer Chest woke him from the dead. . . .

PART ONE

CHAPTER 1

Easter Day, 1883

 It was a moment filled with hope, the moment Daniel was born.

"Not one Hutchinson man has made it to middle age," Joseph whispered into the ear of his sleeping newborn son, "—yet."

Many Hutchinsons married, some started families, all worked the farm, but none made it further than a few years past their twenty-first birthday.

Everyone in the small Long Island town whispered under their breath that it was God's will. Some shuddered, saying it was a curse or the evil eye. Others insisted it was simply plain, old bad luck.

No explanation made sense because the Hutchinsons were the best kind of people you'd ever want to meet. There was nothing they would not do for you, and everyone in town had a story to tell about a good deed done for them by a Hutchinson. But for all their good deeds, in the end, the Hutchinsons could not keep their boys out of harm's way.

On the day Daniel was born, all of his ancestors' unfulfilled dreams shifted onto him. The accumulated hopes of generations were laid upon his innocent shoulders before he had taken the first drink of his mother's milk. Maybe with him the spell would be broken, and the Hutchinson men would live into old age. Joseph Hutchinson was counting on it.

"You have a lot to live up to, Daniel," he said rocking his son in his arms, if indeed he was to live at all.

Joseph's father died at twenty-five years of age. It was a straightforward fall off a horse that should have given him nothing more than some scratches and a good story to tell the children at the noon meal.

"There's no reason for the fall to have taken his life," the doctor had said.

But there it was, he was a Hutchinson, and his time had come.

Ten years later, Joseph inherited the farm from his mother, who had worked so hard to keep it afloat by herself that it was probably more the cause of her fatal illness than the "weak heart" the doctor blamed. Plain and simple, she was worn out.

A week after laying his mother to a well-deserved rest, Joseph took over right where she had left off. He quickly learned that he would not be working the farm; the farm would be working him.

"You had better be strong." Joseph addressed the baby he cradled protectively in his arms, his firstborn son whom he had helped his wife, Miriam, birth twelve hours earlier.

Miriam had not recognized the labor pains that grew worse over the course of the afternoon. She shrugged them off as a bellyache from a bowl of oatmeal too hastily eaten at sunrise. After all, the baby wasn't due for a month.

Moreover, she was preoccupied with her work in the field. Farmwork was exacting; everything was precisely timed in preparation for the harvest. Neither she nor Joseph could afford to take an afternoon off as the land hardly provided enough for them to make it through the year.

It was for this reason that Miriam's mother had pleaded with her not to marry this boy.

Miriam could recite their argument by heart. . . .

"I don't mean to meddle, sweetheart, but if you ask me—"

"But I haven't asked you, Momma," Miriam sighed.

"Honey, Joseph's prospects are dim," she lowered her voice lest she be overheard, "and he's cursed. All the Hutchinson men are. Everyone knows it."

"I don't care about everyone." Miriam was convinced that her love was strong enough to save him from the Hutchinson fate. "Nothing matters but that I love him."

"I'm sure you do. Joseph is a handsome young man, but marriage is for life." She knew that death was only a concept to her daughter; Miriam was still a baby when her father died. But she pressed on anyway. "Who will take care of your children should he—" she searched with care for the next words, "pass unexpectedly?"

"The Bible says that love is stronger than death, Momma. Are you saying that the Bible isn't true?"

"I won't argue the Bible with you—"

"Then maybe you've just forgotten what it

is like to be young." Miriam tried every argument she could think of.

"Don't put me in the grave just yet. I am not that old."

"Joseph has dreams, Momma. One day he's going to be more than a farmer—so much more!"

"I'm all for dreams, Daughter, but it is reality that puts food on the table."

Miriam stopped arguing and put her whole heart into begging. "Please say yes, Mother."

All the women in her family had minds of their own, and her daughter was no different. Yet she couldn't help but smile. For all of Miriam's timidity, once she set her heart on something, it was already hers. "He seems to be a good man, that Joseph Hutchinson."

"Oh, Momma, thank you," she squealed with relief. "From the day I set eyes on him at the county store I knew that he would ask me to marry him." And she knew, too, that she would say yes.

"It sounds like love . . . ," Mother said, drifting back to the moment she had laid eyes on the dashing gentleman with the pencil-thin mustache thirty years her senior who had taken her heart. "Love at first sight."

"Exactly," Miriam exclaimed. Love at first sight is exactly what it was with Joseph Hutchinson. . . .

Miriam was surprised when her water broke in the cornfield, and by the time she reached the house she did not have the strength to make it up the single flight of stairs to her bed. Other than her feather mattress, the Hutchinson farmhouse had little to offer in the way of comfort. Inside, like the outside, was a study in simplicity and efficiency. There was the front room where they sat and the kitchen (with a cellar beneath it) where they ate, with a stone fireplace covering one entire wall. On the second floor there were two bedrooms spacious enough only for sleeping and dressing, and atop that a cramped attic nestled beneath the steeply pitched roof. Miriam lay down on the cushioned bench in the front room and waited for her husband to come and wash up for the noon meal. She could do no more than wait.

She did not have to wait long. Forty minutes later Joseph sauntered into the kitchen, clenching a raggedy bunch of wildflowers in his fist.

"Miriam," he called out, "I have a gift for you." One day he promised himself he'd be able to afford real gifts, not ones stolen from the earth.

Miriam's mother had tried to prepare her for the pain of childbirth, but nonetheless Miriam cried out with the intensity of it. "I'm here."

She did not want to be doubled over in front of Joseph, but the contractions were coming faster and were harder to bear.

Though she was only in the next room, her answer sounded weak and far away. He moved toward her voice, and when he saw her chalky white complexion and her lips drained of color, he ran to her side, dropping the flowers and falling to his knees.

"It's just labor pains, Joseph—" her words cut short by another contraction that shot through her body.

"It can't be. It's a full month early," Joseph explained, as if declaring it made it so. He laid his hands on her swollen belly that felt near about to burst. But what if she was right? He shuddered with an animal fear that all men feel at such a time, when they know they are powerless to stop nature from taking its course. "Miriam, I am telling you it is too early."

She couldn't help but laugh—at seventeen, her husband was still a boy. "Early or not, our baby is coming."

"But, Miriam," he said, trying to reason with her, "you don't understand. There is no time to get the midwife. Even if I fly, I won't return with her in time."

He stood up and began to pace the length of the front room. "What shall we do?" he asked, his voice cracking with emotion.

"You will have to do what has to be done, Joseph." She said it just like that, as if birthing a baby was something Joseph had done just the other day.

He looked at her incredulously.

Miriam knew her man; he was capable of rising to the occasion.

Joseph's panic increased, but he knew she was right. "There's something I must do first, and when I come back, I will be your manly midwife." With something to do he no longer felt powerless.

She smiled at his attempt at humor, envisioning Joseph in an apron doing her bidding.

When Miriam first laid eyes on him in the county store, it was she who was wearing the apron, and she doing his bidding. Naturally, she had heard the gossip about the curse, but here was Joseph standing before her just as handsome as he could be. "Can I help you find what you're looking for?" she asked.

"I think I might've already found it," Joseph responded with more boldness than he knew he possessed. "I'm Joseph Hutchinson," he said, offering his hand.

She took his hand in both of her own as if it were a prize she had just been awarded at the fair.

Her gentle touch urged him on. "Would you like to take a walk with me on Sunday afternoon?"

"I'll have to ask permission from my mother."

"Do you think your mother will like someone like me?" he asked with the confidence of a man twice his age. The last time Joseph was smitten by love he'd lost his senses, but with this girl he seemed to have full do-minion over them. "What do you say?"

"I'll have to let you know. . . ."

"When?"

His forwardness scared her and thrilled her. "Tomorrow?" she stuttered.

The blush coloring her cheeks encour-aged him. "That means I'll have to come back into town tomorrow."

"I suppose it does," Miriam said. "I'm sorry."

"No, you're not! You're not the least bit sorry."

Miriam broke into a glorious smile. She liked him. No, she more than liked him.

Her smile expanded until Joseph felt its warmth envelop him. He, who spent his days beneath the dark Hutchinson cloud, found himself unexpectedly standing in the presence of a bright sun. And it was shining directly upon him.

They stood for a moment, face to face, silently contemplating each other.

Maybe her light was bright enough to burn away the black Hutchinson fate. "Then, I will see you tomorrow, Miss—"

"You may call me Miriam."

"Miriam." The soft vowels felt nice against

his hard life. "Then I'll see you tomorrow, Miriam. And the day after that, and the day after that!"

"That's too much," she said, responding with words more proper than accurate. "What will people think?"

"What they think won't keep me from coming back day after day 'til I'm sure that you won't change your mind about me between now and Sunday."

She sensed that Joseph saw right through to her soul—saw that she would go walking with him on Sunday no matter what her mother said. . . .

Joseph knelt down beside Miriam and took his wife's hands in his own. He pressed them hard, trying to transfer his strength to her. "I will come back," he said. "Just give me a few minutes." Then he stood up and ran out of the front room.

He hurriedly climbed the first flight of stairs, rushing past the two small bedrooms and hall storage cubby and then the final steps to the attic door. He unlocked the plain unpainted pine door with a key that only he possessed and entered the small space that was his refuge, his stronghold.

He locked the door behind him and walked the few steps to the chair in the center of the dimly lit room. He sat down, closed his eyes, and tried to concentrate. But who could concentrate at a time like this?

Without money to pay for a doctor and without time to call on the midwife, Joseph placed the fullness of his faith in this stuffy little attic that had served as his holy temple since the day it answered his first prayer years ago.

When Joseph was a boy living in a house full of Hutchinsons, he shared his small bedroom with two brothers; he had no place to call his own. No sooner had he set his sights on the cellar than his mother declared in a tone that left little room for discussion, "The cellar's no place for a boy."

It was his older brother, Luke, who suggested the attic. "Ma doesn't go up there at all except to pile up stuff that nobody wants." That very day Joseph claimed it as his own and soon he labeled it his "thinking through" place.

Despite the limited space, this attic housed all things Hutchinson—a collection of broken furniture and crates filled with clothes, toys, nonsense, and what-nots. They were all con- secrated artifacts to Joseph; all imbued with the special power that ancient history ac- cords things. It was amidst this history that he found his security in times of need.

One lonely night, on a lark, he prayed to the power of the attic for love, and a few months later he was hired to work on Grace Brown's farm. The attic had answered his prayer. After that Joseph unquestioningly trusted in the power of this room.

"Help me to deliver my firstborn child." His current prayer was simple and to the point.

Only two minutes of silence passed be- fore Joseph said, under his breath, "Thank you," and swiftly exited the room, locking the door behind him. Once outside the door, his wife's cry quickly brought him back to the reality at hand.

Three hours and twenty-two minutes later, his baby boy with black hair and blue eyes was born. Joseph cut the umbilical cord perfectly and left the two of them alone only after they had fallen sound asleep in each other's arms. He tiptoed out of the house to begin his search for the perfect piece of wood. Working with wood brought him happiness and a peace of mind like nothing else. Less so now with the responsibilities of manhood, but when Joseph was younger, there was always a piece of wood for carving in one of his many pockets.

By the time his son's first cry for food and attention and love reached his ears, Joseph had carved his son a toy he knew would delight him. It was a soldier that moved its arms and legs in unison when you pulled the string at the top of his little helmet. But no matter how hard Joseph giggled at the sight of the silly, dancing soldier he dangled before Daniel, the single crease line drawn straight across his forehead, a trademark of all the Hutchinson males, never lessened.

CHAPTER 2

Summer, 1885

Upon fifteen acres of farmland (that was at one time thirty-five) sat the Hutchinson farmhouse. Constructed of wood—pine primarily, with oak used for the shingle siding and roof—it was built simply and sturdily. The foundation and the large chimney were made of stone. A long lean-to porch provided dry space to store the firewood and left enough room for a bench and two rocking chairs upon which to pause and catch one's breath between chores. The square attic window and the small diamond-shaped windows (all with shutters) and the large garden enjoyed the light and warmth of the southern exposure.

Joseph and Miriam were on their knees in the garden picking vegetables for the noon meal. Miriam was days away from birthing their second baby. "I didn't marry you, Joseph, to live a life of luxury."

"I know you didn't, but I thought that with time things would get easier."

"That's because you're a dreamer, Husband," Miriam smiled. "And I would not have it any other way."

"A lot of good my dreaming does us."

While the Hutchinson farm had grown in heart over the years since it was settled by his ancestors, it had shrunk in acreage. One after another of the Hutchinson men had died young, leaving the working of the land to their wives and small children. Each generation either borrowed money against the farm or sold off parcels of land to make ends meet.

Miriam ran a fingertip across Joseph's perennially furrowed brow, leaving behind an earthy smudge. She laughed at her artwork. "Haven't you noticed that it's too beautiful a day to be worrying about anything?"

"A wife big with child on her knees in the garden, and me with a curse over my head. How can I not worry?"

"Will you ever believe me when I tell you that love will prevail?"

"You and your faith," he said, reaching toward her for an embrace. But Daniel's cry from the kitchen took precedence.

Miriam instinctively pulled away. "Our son is hungry, Husband."

"So is his father!" Joseph said playfully to Miriam's back as he watched her disappear into the house.

Joseph Hutchinson returned his thoughts to weeds for a moment before jamming his fists into the soil in frustration. "I wasn't born to be a farmer," he growled resentfully. Not a single moment of his life was his own. The crops dictated his life and ordered his days from sunrise to sundown, season to season. The farm, the farm, always it was the farm that came first.

The following morning at breakfast the Hutchinson men ate their morning meal with unusual gusto: Daniel atop Miriam's lap and Joseph sitting beside her. Joseph loved nothing more than her pan-baked flatbread smothered with warm pumpkin-apple butter. So even though a day of backbreaking work in the fields awaited him, at the moment he was exceedingly happy.

"Are you ready for a visitor today, little one?" Miriam asked her son at her bosom. She tried but could not suppress the hint of a smile upon her lips.

Joseph turned to her. "A visitor?" Sabbath was the day for visitors, not midweek.

"Two visitors, actually—the midwife and our new little girl." No one had to tell Miriam that it was a girl she'd carried these last nine months.

Finally realizing what Miriam was saying, Joseph shot up off his seat knocking his chair backwards onto the floor. He hugged his wife with a suffocating embrace, upsetting his son's breakfast. As Daniel cried at the interruption, Joseph ran upstairs to the bedroom to ready it for Miriam's return. This time their child would come as planned—in the ninth month, in a real bed, and delivered by a real midwife.

When Joseph returned to the kitchen, Miriam was sitting in the rocking chair by the hearth with Daniel asleep in her arms. He hugged her again like there was no tomorrow.

"Just go, Husband, unless you want to birth our daughter," she threatened playfully.

Once was enough for him, Joseph said, with a big-hearted laugh. He took off to the barn and, without saddling up Eleanor, jumped atop the mare and rode her bareback into town.

When he arrived at the house of the midwife, it was her husband who opened the door. Without introducing himself, Joseph's news poured forth from his lips in one endless sentence. The man slapped him on the back and promised that his wife would be out to his homestead before noon.

"She's not here now?" Joseph was stunned. "I thought she'd follow me back home in her carriage."

"She's attending the birth of the Baxter babe," the husband explained, matching none of Joseph's urgency.

"What if the birth takes longer than—"

"Don't worry, man, you have my word."

"Your word?" Joseph echoed, full of fear now.

"I promise you," the husband said with a hint of impatience, "she'll be there by noon."

They went back and forth like this several times before Joseph yielded, though he was not a bit reassured, knowing no man on earth could predict the time of a baby's birth.

———

Miriam's labor pains began in earnest at two o'clock. By three, the midwife had not yet arrived. By four, Joseph was in a frenzy. What if she forgot? What if she didn't come? He ran downstairs to the kitchen and walked in circles, unable to control his terror. When he threw open the door to begin searching the roads, he bumped into her on the porch.

"The Baxter baby came feet first, Mr. Hutchinson. It was a difficult delivery," she stammered nervously. "I apologize for my husband's overconfidence. A woman would never have made you such a promise."

"You were afraid of losing your job, and I was afraid of having to do it," Joseph managed, with a feeble smile.

Relieved at his unexpected humor, the woman replied, "I guess that makes us even."

Not quite even, he thought, but said instead, "Tell me, what can I do to help you?"

"You can give my horse something to drink, and leave your wife and me alone. But before you do, a cup of tea would be nice."

This said, she took charge of the household with a sharp, professional air. She removed her hat and gloves and laid her thick carpetbag on the floor. Without asking Joseph's permission, she added two pieces of wood to the fire in the hearth for added warmth. She then neatly wrapped herself in a crisp white apron that would soon take on the crimson color of the new baby's birth.

Joseph spied her actions while making her tea. Then he made his way quietly up the stairs to the bedroom and to Miriam, who was in a welcome moment of peace between contractions.

"May I come in?" he asked shyly.

Miriam answered by opening her arms to him. While her husband grew meeker during these times of crisis, she grew bolder.

Three-quarters of an hour later, while Daniel napped, Joseph climbed the stairs to the attic. He unlocked the door and stepped into the darkened room rich with the possessions of his ancestors. He had never told Miriam just how important the attic was to him. How could he explain what he felt in this room?

He went first, as he always did, to the Hutchinson family Bible. But it was not the

Bible that interested him. Unlike Miriam, Joseph was not a believer. It was the first twenty-three pages that housed the personal births and deaths, accomplishments, and noteworthy anecdotes. These introductory pages were sacred to Joseph. The book had been in the family as long as anyone could remember. The fragile binding threatened to give way each time Joseph opened the cover, but because he handled it as tenderly as he had his infant son on the day he was born, it remained intact despite its age.

Joseph took a seat on the chair in the center of this tiny room and held the book lovingly on his lap, stroking the cover as he might a lucky rabbit's foot. The chair, as old as the house itself, was missing two back spindles, the front right leg was loose, and the back left one a bit shorter than the others. As to its original painted color, one could only guess. But it was a different kind of comfort that Joseph was after.

He closed his eyes and sat in silence. Certainly he heard the increasing moans of his wife downstairs, but they did not touch him up here in his attic.

Miriam explained to him time and again

that all power comes from God, not a room crammed with things. But Joseph knew better. He knew that God lived up in the sky, not on earth or in his home where Joseph needed Him most. The attic, on the other hand, was always at the top of the stairs; it was tangible, something he could touch and hold on to, something he could pray to that was close enough to listen, and answer. Over the years the attic became his god, and Joseph put his unconditional trust in its absolute power.

Time stood still in this room as he prayed, so when he exited the attic, there was no telling if a minute or an hour had passed. It must have been quite a while, for immediately upon locking the door behind him he was met with his wife's agonizing cries from the floor below.

He raced down the stairs and returned to her bedside and the urgent matter at hand, the birth of his scrawny little daughter, whom they named Mary. She kept her mother up that first night making the funniest faces. She was a character right from the start.

Joseph spent the night in the barn making a beautiful pony out of the sweetest honey-colored wood that he'd been saving for a special occasion. The delightfully long blond mane and tail were made of fine threads he'd stolen from Miriam's sewing box. One day I may be able to give her a real pony, he daydreamed. But he wouldn't love the animal any more than the one in the palm of his hand, the one that he himself had brought to life. Its compassionate eyes, legs that moved, and tail that swished made it seem almost real. Such was the skill and the love that Joseph possessed for wood-working.

CHAPTER 3

Six years later, June 1891

It would be out of the question to re-count the hundreds of small changes that transpired over the years. Daniel and Mary grew inch by inch, as did Joseph's pleasure in their company.

There were moments, such as the time late one afternoon when the children found him in the fields and insisted that he play with them. "Sure I will," he answered, as if there was nothing more important to him than building a rock fortress with them. Or the night the cast-iron stove belched out so much smoke that Joseph decided to make a tent for the four of them so they could sleep outdoors under the stars. Or the morning at the end of January when his family had the snowball fight to end all snowball fights.

No sooner was Joseph in the door at sun-down than the children would offer up sto-ries they had written, or fights for him to resolve, or wounds for him to kiss. Daniel and Mary had Joseph's undivided attention.

Joseph and Miriam grew, too, into a deep comfort with each other. They entered into the private language of married couples, where a quiet gaze could replace a sentence and a silence could communicate a story. After the children were tucked into bed for the night came the sweetest time of all, the precious hour or two entirely their own.

Miriam wished her mother could see how well things turned out for them; they worked hard and in return God's abundance was everywhere present. She finished stacking the pewter plates, gave her husband a goodbye kiss, and then reached for her overcoat.

Joseph watched her prepare to leave. "Are you going to care for Rose again?" Joseph asked, knowing full well that lately Miriam spent one night a week with her neighbor Grace's four-year-old daughter.

"Where else would I be going after sundown, Joseph?" she laughed at him. "To the dance hall in town?"

He did not want her to go, so he made a joke of it. "Another man perhaps? What husband can say for certain what goes through his woman's mind? They say the ninth year of marriage is the trickiest, Wife."

She could feel his love in his words. "Well then, Husband, here's a trick for you. Saddle up Eleanor for me so I can arrive at Grace's before midnight."

Rose Brown was a sickly baby from the start, but in Miriam's arms her sufferings seemed to soften, her temperature cooled, she even breathed easier. While Joseph admired his wife's faith, it troubled him. He rose from the rocking chair by the hearth and moved towards her. He took her face in his hands. "If you could," he asked, "you would take Rose's ills upon yourself, wouldn't you?"

The man could still see right through her. "Would that I had the power to do it, Joseph."

It was not at all what he wanted to hear. With a flash of anger, he said, "I forbid it, Miriam. Maybe your faith can heal the world, but what good will it do me if I lose my wife and the children their mother?" He turned and walked toward the door.

"Joseph, my dear husband—" she said, surprised by the outburst, but knowing it was hopeless to argue with him. Her faith had always been a source of disagreement between them; this argument was nothing new. "You know that I cannot bear to watch a child suffer."

Wasn't it enough that he was cursed, did she have to follow him to the grave? "Then why must we bear it when the suffering of some neighbor's child becomes our own?" He gripped the door handle hard enough to turn his knuckles white.

"She is not just some neighbor, Joseph. She is Grace Brown, your old friend."

He had long ago shut the door on that part of his life. He turned abruptly to face her and said, "And you, Miriam Hutchinson, are my wife." He grabbed his hat from the iron hook by the door and added, "Let me tell you what your problem is. You are too good, and one day I fear it will be the death of you."

With this he banged out of the front door, fuming all the way to the barn. As he pulled the harness on Eleanor, he remembered when he was fourteen and how the mere mention of Grace's name sent shivers down his spine. . . .

It had been on a Friday that Joseph climbed the porch steps with his heart banging away in his chest and knocked excitedly on the Brown's front door. He knew Grace would answer because Mr. Brown was never around. People said her husband married her to get his hands on her family's money. They said that he loved his drink more than his wife. Joseph could not believe a man could love anything more than Grace. With her pale blond hair worn wild and loose and her cornflower blue eyes, Joseph imagined her on stage. He dreamt of her during his restless and solitary nights, performing just for him. He was in love with her, as only a fourteen-year-old boy could be. Incurably. Desperately. Silently.

"Hello there," Grace said cordially, opening the door to him. She had the coins counted out, ready to pay him.

Joseph lived for Fridays. No other day of the week held a speck of meaning other than that it drew him one day closer to Friday, the day he spent doing chores on the Brown farm. Joseph extended his hand, and Grace passed the coins from her palm to his.

The weight of the twelve coins made

Joseph feel like a real man. "Thank you, Mrs. Brown," he said in his deepest voice.

Utterly unlike that of her own husband, Joseph's young passion was palpable, and a spark of it ignited within her. "You're welcome," she responded, and quite unexpectedly reached out to stroke his cheek.

At the touch of her fingertips, Joseph's ears turned bright crimson. Trapped in his prison of infatuation, unable to articulate even one of his feelings, he began to stammer.

Flattered, but conflicted, Grace immediately withdrew her hand. With immense tenderness, she said, "You'll know that you've met the right woman for you when the words flow freely from your lips."

But I have met the right woman, he ached to say, and here she stands before me! Joseph pressed on despite the fact that his palms were sweating and his mouth felt like sand. "Grace," he stuttered, "I have to t-t-tell you how much I . . ."

While the county doctor prescribed cool baths and bed rest for little Rose, Miriam stuck to her own prescription. "Love," she said to Grace. "Love is the cure for everything."

But there came a day when Rose's breathing grew distressed, and she would not eat. She was struggling to survive.

Though it kept her awake through the night, Miriam waited until sunrise to talk to Joseph about Rose's worsening condition. "You know that Grace has had more than her share of hardship. You heard the gossip—while Grace was with child her husband ran off with that Becky Stone, who shared his love for drink. Grace put up a good front for the sake of the neighbors, Joseph, but how could a woman not take something like that to heart?" All this was her way of saying that it would be downright heartless not to help her.

How could Miriam have guessed the depth of Joseph's feelings for Grace when he had buried them so deeply within himself. . . .

Young Joseph had no experience in matters of the heart. Face-to-face with Grace he simply could not stop stuttering.

Grace put her fingertips to his lips and smiled. "Sssh, now, Joseph."

His eyes burned with the need to share his feelings. He had to, he just had to.

Perhaps it was because of their dark fate that the Hutchinson men had an intensity well beyond their years. Grace felt the rising force of it and took two steps back. She dared not look him directly in the eyes any longer, so it was Mrs. Grace Brown who brought the conversation to a close. "One day it'll be different, Joe. I promise you."

With the thought that she was speaking about the two of them, Joseph vowed, "I will hold you to that promise."

Then two years later he met Miriam and found that to his surprise the words flowed easily from his lips, just as Grace had predicted.

With her hands resting on her hips, Miriam stared at her husband awaiting his reply. "What say you, Husband?"

"I say that we must do what we can to help Grace and her daughter."

Through an audible sigh of relief, Miriam told Joseph that she wanted to spend the nights with Rose.

"How many nights?" he asked, willing to compromise somewhat.

"Every night," she said, holding her breath.

"You're asking me to sleep alone?"

"Only for a week, maybe two, until Rose's condition improves."

"Doing a kindness is one thing, Miriam. But your kindness knows no bounds."

"Grace is family, Joseph. Or have you forgotten? She offered you much kindness when you were a boy."

Joseph remained silent.

"And there is something else. With you in the fields by day and me at Rose's side at night, Daniel should be given charge of Mary," Miriam suggested, expertly changing the topic.

It took some doing for Joseph to hold his tongue, but he held it for Miriam, who was no longer the shy, sheltered girl he had courted; she had blossomed into a bold woman with a mind of her own.

The next morning Miriam broke the news to Daniel that he was to be the man of the family in her absence. As expected, Daniel beamed and Mary sulked.

"Don't worry, Momma, I will take good care of my baby sister."

"I'm not a baby," Mary cried, turning to Miriam for sympathy.

Miriam and Joseph laughed, but to Mary this was no laughing matter. It was not Daniel's directions she resisted, for she knew the chores he assigned her had to be done. It was the way in which he relished bossing her around that irked her.

Miriam slept in Rose's bed with the little girl in her arms for two weeks before a healthy blush returned to her cheeks. It was a blush that Rose had never had, even since birth, as if all the sickliness she was born with was gone, as if she was somehow born anew.

Miriam returned to her own family, however, in noticeably diminished health. An uncontrollable cough now plagued her. The honey teas the children made for her could not tame it, and the hours spent inhaling steam from the boiling kettle offered only temporary relief.

The doctor assured them that Rose's sickness was not contagious. "Miriam, it's the strain of having taken care of two families for two weeks," he explained, suggesting warm baths and bed rest. Had he not been so inexperienced with symptoms of pneumonia, he would have known that neither soaking in an ocean of baths nor drinking a sea of tea would help Miriam's lungs. "Give it time," he repeated. "It will pass."

Every morning, rain or shine, Grace traveled the three miles to bring Miriam a basket overflowing with wonderful, still-warm, home-baked breads and nourishing broths.

Miriam could not relieve Grace of her guilt, nor convince her that she did not regret a moment of her time spent with Rose.

Joseph, on the other hand, regretted it plenty.

CHAPTER 4

Three weeks later, July

Twenty-one long and arduous days and nights into Miriam's coughing sickness, Joseph unlocked the attic door. He sat for a long time in silence, praying to the magic of the attic. "Make Miriam better, and make my life go back to the way it was." The prayer was not meant to be fancy, just clear.

By the time he fell asleep later that night he was confident that tomorrow everything would be different.

It was high noon, and Joseph was laboring out in the fields, his throat parched and his neck burned beet red. The sun was blinding, so when Joseph saw something shimmering in the distance he could not entirely trust his eyes. Let it be a cool pitcher of water to quench my thirst, he wished. A few tentative steps in its direction and he could see that it was really a wooden box—a chest, but unlike any other he had ever seen. With his love of carpentry Joseph understood the perfection of such an artistic creation.

The chest was ancient, but meticulously maintained. Across the length of its lid was cut a rectangular slot in which to slip letters, Joseph guessed, or perhaps important papers. The entire surface of the wood was ornately carved with symbols that Joseph recognized but could not identify. It could have been a ceremonial chest used for religious purposes, but Joseph could not say for sure.

Of one thing only was he certain: it was too beautiful to have been fashioned by human hands. The silvery hardware gleamed with the patina of many hundreds, perhaps thousands of years of age and polish. Most surprisingly of all, a tiny lock shone brightly against the backdrop of the rich, dark wood, a lock made of pure gold.

As Joseph got closer and his eyes accustomed themselves to the bright surroundings, he could see more clearly through the light that there were hands holding the box—hands so pearly white, they were practically translucent. Beside himself with curiosity, Joseph reached out to touch the chest, maybe even take it and make it his own. But no sooner had he reached for it than he saw whose hands held this mysterious box: they were the hands of an angel! She leaned toward him and whispered, "God is real, Joseph."

Joseph could not understand what he was seeing and hearing.

"I have come to take something from you," she said smiling serenely, "and give you something far greater in return."

In a horrifying flash of realization that knocked the wind out of him, Joseph understood: Here was the Angel of Death standing before him offering this chest in return for his life. "Taking my father and brothers wasn't enough for you? Do you think I'm stupid enough to exchange my life for some chest?" he growled. *"Why don't you take someone else instead!"* he spat the words from his lips as if they were poison, and when he lunged at the Angel of Death he had every intention of choking the ghastly life out of her. . . .

Joseph awoke and jumped up in a panic, panting like a frightened animal. Enveloped in the blackness of the night, he stood at the

foot of his bed wavering: was it a horrible
dream? It felt real as rain, but it was a
dream, wasn't it? Telling himself it couldn't
be real but unable to shake the image of the
angel, he tore out of the bedroom leaving
Miriam behind. Wearing only his nightshirt,
he ran barefoot down the steps and through
the kitchen, knocking over two stools and
the pile of firewood. He raced out the door
and off the porch and began running full-out
toward the fields, chased by his curse.

"You can't catch me!" he yelled. Somehow he felt that if he won this race, he'd live
another day; if he lost, the sickle of death
would claim yet another Hutchinson.

"Take someone else instead of me," he
screamed like a madman, flying across the
fields. "I don't want to die!"

He tore right through the creek bed that
adjoined his property to the Browns', and
the shock of the icy water brought him to
his senses. Joseph stopped. Only now did
he realize that it was the middle of the night,
and he was standing barefoot next to a
creek wearing only his nightshirt.

The burden of fear every Hutchinson man
carried pressed down on him until he sank
to his knees. He was no match for the Angel

of Death. Shaking from the dream and the cold and the wet earth, he hurled his fury at the sky, "I'm only twenty-five. It's not fair!"

Then, for the first time in his young life, Joseph buried his face in his earth-darkened hands and cried bitterly for the loss of his two brothers. He traveled back to the darkest day of his life, the day that he lost both of them and ended his special time with Grace. . . .

It was on one of his special Fridays when Joseph was digging a series of trenches to irrigate Grace's fields that a secret fever, like a black cat in the night, silently crept through the Hutchinson house. The pity of it was, nothing you did made a difference. On the first day, it took its victims into a half-sleep from which they never awoke; on the second, it took them all the way into eternal sleep. That Saturday it took his older brother Luke and his younger brother Paul. The loss tore his heart in two as easily as if it were made of paper. His mother had told him he shouldn't complain—he should be grateful for who remained.

Well, he was complaining now. He cried a river of bitter tears and sent his long overdue curses upward into the unresponsive night sky.

At the break of dawn, when he heard the chirping of the birds, he bent over the creek bed and splashed handfuls of the cool water on his face, trying to wash away any trace of emotion. As a Hutchinson he had reason to fear the Angel of Death, but even so his fear shamed him. "You can keep your damn chest."

Then he stood up feeling stronger, taller even, and walked purposefully toward home. All of a sudden he was ravenous for food and his wife and his life. He was alive. This Hutchinson man had outwitted fate yet another day.

CHAPTER 5

Morning

Joseph threw open the door expecting to see his wife by the stove preparing his breakfast, awaiting his return. He was cocky with his reprieve from death, selfish even.

"Did you not think your husband would return hungry?" he called out into the silent house.

There was so much to be done at daybreak, and this morning not one thing had even been started. He noticed the overturned stools and firewood still strewn on the floor, the table was bare, the stove cold. "Miriam, where are you?" he said, with obvious irritation.

In response he heard strange muffled sounds coming from the second-floor. He followed the sound up the stairs.

When he reached the threshold of his bedroom door his blood froze.

Miriam lay in their bed exactly as he had left her hours before, but Daniel was tugging her arm. Staring at her lifeless figure, he realized that the angel that had come to take him was forced to take Miriam instead. If only he had not insisted that the Angel take someone else. If only he had accepted the Hutchinson fate like a man.

If only . . . if only . . . the doubts screamed inside his own mind. Each word was a hot coal he forced himself to swallow until he felt his soft heart harden into something heavy and black, like the granite stones he used for building walls. Grief and anger and craziness eclipsed all logic.

But he dared show none of this to his children. The children. Only now did he hear their cries. Daniel was pleading, "Wake up, Momma. Wake up." Mary was crumpled on the floor sobbing. They turned to Joseph with miserable tear-streaked faces and one overarching question they could not answer, "Why won't Momma wake up?"

Joseph reached out to Miriam and stroked her hair, her forehead, her cold cheeks. Then he turned to his children and grabbed them up into his arms. He who once called himself a good father, a good husband, a good man felt he could call himself these things no more.

"Momma's gone to heaven," Joseph offered feebly.

"But why, Poppa?" Mary asked.

"Because God was lonely, sweetheart." He did not know what else to say. Joseph hugged his children against him, as if holding them tight might keep them safe from harm. They sobbed into his broad chest, soaking his nightshirt with their endless tears.

"But now *we* will be lonely, Poppa," Daniel managed to say through his tears.

Mary climbed up onto her parents' bed and motioned for her father and brother to do the same. Holding Miriam's hands, each whispering a long goodbye, the dam burst, and their tears went from stream to river to ocean with no end in sight.

CHAPTER 6

A few hours later

When they could cry no more, they had to eat, so the Hutchinsons pushed down some dry bread and milk.

In the dark July morning, Joseph dressed his children in their Sunday clothes and hats. He walked out of the house wearing his nightshirt, still damp with their sorrow, hastily tucked into his overalls. The wind whipped from the ocean to the east; there was a nasty summer thunderstorm brewing.

Ordinarily, the music of the birds calling to one another would have delighted them, but today, trapped inside their own private wells of loneliness, they did not hear it. Hand-in-hand-in-hand, Joseph walked with the children in silence toward Grace Brown's farm three miles to the west.

Joseph knocked on his neighbor's door with a force that frightened his children. Grace opened the door tentatively—the intensity of the knock had scared her, too. Seeing Joe with his little ones at this most unusual time of the morning was not a good sign. "Why . . . come in, Joe dear," she said, a little unsure.

He sent the children inside in his stead. They went straight over to Rose and despite her sadness, Mary began mothering Rose, giving her the comfort she herself needed to receive.

Joseph had never asked for help since he was old enough to bathe himself, but he asked Grace for it now. Without it he could not help Miriam, and it was for her that he had come.

Stifling all trace of emotion, he said the words plainly. "Miriam passed away in the night."

"Oh, Joe," Grace cried out.

A surprising burst of Rose's laughter that emerged from the house underscored the reality that Miriam was dead, and Rose was very much alive. On any other day the sound of Rose's laughter would have brought a smile to Grace's face. "I'm so sorry, Joe, you have no idea—"

Joseph recoiled from the comfort of Grace's outstretched arms. "There is so much to do," he interrupted, "and with the children afoot I can't—"

"Hush, Joe," she soothed. "Hush."

He clenched his fists against the rising tide of his tears and would not let Grace's soft words console him for a death that was his own fault.

"You know I loved your Miriam. She was a blessing to my Rose. Of course, I'll help you take care of the children, and whatever else you need."

Grace Brown knew all too well how many things there were to be done with a stone-cold body in the house. She had buried her grandfather, Elijah, just eight years back. "You know that Miriam's mother needs to know." Grace had kept in touch with her after she moved up north to care for her ailing sister.

"You tell her," Joseph said.

"I'll do whatever you ask, Joe, you know that. Just ask." Grace would write the letter this very afternoon. There was no fate worse than outliving your child, and Miriam had saved Grace from that fate.

Joseph thanked her for her kindness but did not so much as take her hand to shake it for fear of breaking down.

Torn between what he needed and what he needed to do, he turned to go, leaving his children behind and heading toward the house that was no longer a home.

CHAPTER 7

That afternoon

Once back on his land, Joseph made his way directly to the barn. He did not go to the house, to Miriam. He could not face her yet. He could not face himself.

He flung open the double doors and walked like a man possessed to the large bin that housed the farm utensils. He tore into the neat pile, sending the field mice scurrying and upsetting Eleanor. Pitchforks and hoes, some good, some cracked or rusted through; spare pieces of wood fencing; gardening implements were hurled in all directions until he uncovered what he had long ago buried there.

Buried but not forgotten. Joseph lifted up the sawdust-covered rucksack stuffed with woodworking tools. The heft of it and the heavenly smell of wood shavings brought a light to his eyes.

Once Joseph had dreamed of being a carpenter.

When he was a young boy, the most wonderful afternoons were spent with his Grandpa Elijah carving animals out of pieces from his father's wood pile. Of course Elijah wasn't his real grandpa, for no Hutchinson man lived to see his grandchildren. Grandpa Elijah was Grace's grandfather, on loan to Joseph on whatever afternoons he could spare.

Grandpa Elijah taught him how to be still and listen to the wood whisper what it wanted to become. Some pieces asked to be something important like a table at which to eat breakfast or a rocking chair to rest on at the end of a long day; some wanted a useful purpose but had smaller hopes, like a soupspoon, a tinder box, a cutting board, a shoehorn. And for the unusual and oddest-shaped pieces of wood, he fashioned the most fanciful of destinies—a heart for a redheaded girl whose name he no longer remembered, a game of squares, knick-knacks in the shape of animals carved solely to delight the eye or bring a giggle to a baby's lips.

To him, wood was not a dead thing; it was alive. From the time he was old enough to talk, it absorbed his attention, but life kept getting in the way. First his father passed unexpectedly, making his assistance on the farm more important than ever. He was only a boy of five, but a little boy could do lots of little chores, and there was seemingly no end to them. Then his brothers were stricken with the fever that left just him and his mother. A week before his mother passed away, she made him promise to keep the farm in the family.

"Promise me," she said, "no matter what, you won't let the farm go."

"I promise, Momma. I promise," he repeated until she believed him.

But the price of keeping his promise was letting go of his dream of becoming a carpenter, which felt like yet another death in the family.

Joseph shook the memory loose. His dream died—so what? So had everything and everyone in his life. He grabbed the axe from its leather sheath and stomped to the back of the barn and began chopping away at the barn siding with all the rage and grief and guilt he dared not show his children. But his madness had a purpose. If he had to bury his wife, he would do so with familiar wood that was part of her loving farm, not some wood that meant nothing to her. Joseph knew how Miriam loved this barn. They made love more than once in the barn since they were married; for all her properness while they were dating, the married Miriam loved the impropriety of it. It was so rough, so masculine in the barn that it fanned the flames of her passion. In fact, it was on their wedding night . . .

Miriam swung open the barn door, balancing a mug of steaming tea on a tray. She expected to find Joseph racing to finish up for the night, but instead he was brushing Eleanor down, his beloved mare, as if he had all the time in the world. She couldn't help but laugh. "Are you planning to spend your wedding night with Eleanor?"

"My goodness, Mrs. Hutchinson," he said casually, as if his fingers were not trembling beneath Eleanor's auburn-colored mane. "Are you jealous?"

"I most certainly am. But now that I see my competition, I can safely say that I smell far more pleasant than old Eleanor does."

Her talk made Joseph's hands tremble all the more. "I am sure you do, Wife. But in the future you can't call Eleanor old," he teased, "because she is very sensitive about her age."

Eleanor wasn't the only animal left on the Hutchinson farm, but she was the one he loved most. The cow and the few pigs and chickens served a purpose, whereas Eleanor, somewhere along the way, stopped being just a mare and turned into a member of the family.

"Your history with Eleanor makes her more of a threat to our marriage than I thought," Miriam laughed. "Let's see who the better woman is," she said leaning into him and softly placing her lips upon his. It wasn't their first kiss, but it was their first as a married couple, and for that reason it was unlike any other they'd shared.

Miriam pulled back far enough to whisper, "Can Eleanor do that?"

Once ignited, their excitement could not be postponed. The bedroom felt as far away as the stars in the sky. Instead they fell into a tangle of desire on the barn floor. Despite the discomfort and the smell and the awkwardness and the cold, they made love there all night long. . . .

And now he was burying her, his sweet Miriam. There was no stopping Joseph's tears—he chopped blindly until he could lift the axe no more, until his hands were raw. He gathered the wood siding into a single pile in the center of the barn and sat down on a low stool to "listen" to the wood as Grandpa Elijah called it. It did not take long for the vision to unfold: the coffin was to be plain; on its lid he was to carve a large, beautiful circle, a symbol of God's eternal love for Miriam; and within the circle a cross, simple and pure in its lines.

It made sense to him at once, for on the very day he met Miriam, he spent half that night carving a circle with a perfect cross inside of it for Miriam to wear on a ribbon around her neck. The next day Joseph ran all the way back to the store and presented it to her. Miriam wore it still.

The coffin took most of the day to build, mostly because Joseph's tears, continually wetting the wood, slowed the exacting work of the engraving.

When the task was complete, Joseph carried the pine box into the front room and laid it atop two stools. The box was a weathered red, marked by time and streaked black and brown with the impact of insects and the seasons. It was well lived in, and Miriam would be at home in it.

Joseph knew what the next terrible right action was. He climbed the stairs to his bedroom to face his Miriam. He approached her lifeless body, and with deep shame uttered these words, "Had it not been for me . . ." They both knew the end to the sentence; Miriam had paid dearly for his betrayal.

Joseph lifted her motionless body into his arms. He walked down the stairs and into the front room and delicately, preciously laid his wife in her final resting place. "I'm so sorry, Miriam. . . ."

Joseph looked to see if her body lay comfortably in the confines of the box, but he did not linger. He turned and went to the front porch, grabbing the shovel and heading out toward the elm tree. Planted on the day Daniel came into the world, it would now offer shelter to Miriam as she left this world.

By sundown Joseph was done digging. He would have jumped into the freshly dug grave were it not for the distant voices of his neighbors making their way toward his home.

CHAPTER 8

That night

The night he buried Miriam was the longest night of his life.

He sat on the cushioned bench silent as a stone surrounded by well-meaning friends beseeching him to eat. A plate of food placed beside him went untouched. Faces of neighbors blurred past him: women offering to care for his children and men to tend his fields, and each with a story to tell about Miriam's generosity. He could look none of them in the eye. "It's his grief," they whispered, but it wasn't. It was his shame.

His friends and neighbors went home a few hours before sunrise, leaving behind two weeks worth of food and sympathy.

Grace was slow to go. She cleared the plates, set the slops aside for the animals, swept the floor, and stopped only when she could think of nothing more that needed doing. Only then did she join Joseph on the bench.

She sat beside him in perfect stillness until the first rays of the sun illuminated his front room. She did not want to leave him in the dark.

"Grace," he sighed, staring out the window at the elm tree. It was a plea for help, but Joseph would never admit it.

"Joe, you did everything you could."

Joseph knew better.

"There was nothing anyone could have done."

"It should have been me in the box, not Miriam."

"Joe, let me take Daniel and Mary home with me for the next few weeks."

"No," he barked. "I will not let them down the way I did my wife."

"Stop it, Joe. You loved Miriam. You love her still."

"Grace, you don't understand. It's my fault that she died."

"This is your grief talking, Joe, and I am not listening to it. You shouldn't either. It will do you no good." Grace stood up to go.

He did not turn to her.

"My dear Joe, sometimes you have to let

things fall apart," she said, leaning over to place an innocent kiss on his troubled brow, "for them to come back together again."

He never took his eyes off the elm tree.

She climbed the flight of stairs to the children's bedroom where Rose slept soundly between Daniel and Mary. They awoke when she entered. Grace embraced the three of them with equal love as if they were all her children. She lifted the yawning Rose into her arms and leaned into Joe's children to kiss them each goodbye for now. "In time all will be well," she said. "You'll see."

Of course they could not have heard her right, and Mary told her so, so Grace repeated it. "Believe me, my darlings. All will be well in time."

Grace knew that they could not believe it yet, but they would once Joe did. It was for him that she would be praying.

CHAPTER 9

The next morning

When Grace finally left at sunrise, Joseph immediately climbed the stairs to the attic. He had prayed to the power of the attic before, and his modest prayers had been answered. But what good were the countless little answered prayers in the face of the one unanswered prayer that was more important than them all? Only a fool would have put his unconditional trust into a room, believing that it held special powers. With each step he took, his anger at the attic's betrayal of him increased. He unlocked the door and stepped inside the tiny room.

He closed the door behind him. While the room was dark, Joseph could see things more clearly now. He saw the attic for what it was: ancient cobwebs covering every surface; a drafty four-paned window permanently shut, trapping the air inside, turning it dank and stale; rough wood on the walls and ceilings discolored by dampness.

Why hadn't he seen it before? This room was nothing more than a neglected, cluttered jumble of junk that nobody wanted. Stuff piled high everywhere, broken, useless, passed down year after year rather than being thrown away. His brother Luke had told him as much, but he did not listen.

"There's no magic in this room," he hissed. "Just lies."

A rising storm of ugly emotions gathered force within him. How could he have been so blind? Thankfully, his father and brothers were not here to witness his abject failure as a man. Devilish thoughts went round and round, tormenting him, blaming him, hammering him down until he collapsed onto the dirty, threadbare rug in the center of the room. The years of disappointment, death, and bone-crushing work engulfed him in an uncontrollable rage at the attic, at his fate, at himself.

"What an idiot." He could not leave this room, and he could not stay. His breathing grew ragged like a man drowning in an ocean of self-loathing. Without thinking he grabbed the first wooden crate within reach and hoisted it above his head. With a snarl more beast than human, he hurled it out the attic window. The noise of the shattering glass was satisfying.

"The hell with you!" he yelled out the window, watching it crash to the earth. Joseph began to breathe easier.

He turned back to the room and heaved a small, broken side table up off the floor with a loud grunt and threw it through the shattered window as well. "What good are you if you can't even save my wife?"

Dozens of crates stuffed with outgrown and unworn infant clothes, unused quilts, scraps for mending, broken oil lamps, stubs of candles, and on, and on, item by item, he cast the contents of the attic out the window. "Lies, all lies!"

Lifting the chair above his head, the Hutchinson Bible thudded to the floor beside his feet, startling him. He stood motionless and stared down at the page it fell open to—the family tree. The attic was now empty, everything out the window, except the cloth-bound Hutchinson Bible at his feet and the chair which he held in his hands above his head.

Slowly, he returned the chair to the floor and sat down on it. He picked up the Bible and set it on his lap. "I'm going to have to write

Miriam's death in this," was his first clear thought. That's when the tears came. First one or two, then a downpour: they splashed on the page blurring the names of Hutchinson ancestors. He could not stop them from falling.

He could not close the book. He could not move a muscle. A quarter hour passed until he was numb and as empty as the attic.

Joseph left the attic and went outside. With a callous smile upon his lips, he stood with a piece of lit kindling between his fingertips and stared at the pile. Everything there was a reminder of his life's betrayals: brothers who died without saying goodbye, a father who left him, a mother who forced him to turn away from his love of wood to work the farm, and a wife who stole away in the night, leaving him alone with two little children. When the lit kindling landed on the pile of Hutchinson rubbish, it exploded into a consuming blaze.

The children, who had clung to each other for strength in the kitchen, finally ventured outside. The look in their father's eyes scared them. They stood and watched at a distance.

An hour later, as the last flames settled to glowing embers, Joseph cynically pronounced, "The End." The story of his life was over.

PART TWO

CHAPTER 10

October 29, 1891

Joseph would not set foot in the attic again, and neither would anyone else. "Only lies live up in the attic." His tone of finality let it be known that the topic was no longer open for discussion.

In the months that followed Miriam's death, Joseph went through the motions of his life more like a mechanical toy soldier than a man. He spoke to the children only when necessary: what to eat, when to sleep, what chores needed doing. What was really essential went unspoken—the love Daniel and Mary had for their father and the love they all had for Miriam, how much the children missed her, and how much they needed him to love them. But the children decided not to speak of their needs for fear of upsetting him.

"He needs us to be strong now," Daniel explained to Mary.

In the past they could go to their father for any reason, knowing he would give them his full attention, whether to hear a silly story or to report a fight they had had with each other. There was no burden he did not help them carry. Now they had to help him carry his. Their Poppa's body was in the house but some important part of him was missing, and they labored over this problem nightly.

Daniel explained it to Mary this way, "Poppa put a piece of his heart in the box with Momma to keep her company."

"What's that got to do with why he's acting so funny?"

"It's because a piece of him is not here anymore."

"How can we get it back?"

Daniel slowly shook his head.

So when Mary offered her plan, "What if we love him harder?" he agreed instantly.

They tried climbing on his lap to give him a double hug; they tried reading poems that they wrote for him; they declared their feelings for him openly, saying, "I love you, Poppa," all of which used to make his heart skip a beat. Now, Joseph smiled absentmindedly and turned away. Their love could not touch him.

"Poppa's feelings ran away from home," Mary observed. Daniel could not have explained it better.

With the failure of their original plan, they decided to forge a new one—they were going to leave Poppa alone. They wanted him to be happy, and they thought maybe if they were good—very good—that that would make him happy again. But they were so good at being good that nearly overnight Joseph's children transformed into adults, fathering and mothering him, sacrificing their happiness for his. Weeks passed in this way, and still they saw no change in their father.

Daniel and Mary did their best thinking at night under the covers. They refused to be discouraged. "Maybe," Mary offered, "if we remember something that Poppa used to love doing, it will help."

"That's it," Daniel cried out, reaching across the bed to kiss her. "So, what did Poppa love?"

"He loved Momma and he loved us."

"Think harder."

"I remember! He liked making corncakes for us when it snowed in the morning, and he told Momma to sleep late when she was coughing."

"That's a good one. And how about when Poppa ran a race with us around the barn? Remember how he laughed 'til his stomach hurt?"

If Poppa had laughed or smiled or even shown a glint of light in his eye, it was enough for them to place the memory up for consideration. They thought and thought, until finally he stumbled upon it. "Remember how Poppa would go upstairs to the attic and come down feeling better?"

Mary said that she sort of remembered, which of course meant she didn't.

"Momma said it was his special place," Daniel recounted. "Maybe that's why he kept it locked, to keep the specialness to himself."

"Then why did Poppa tell us that lies live in the attic?"

They both had to think about this one for a minute, because neither wanted to remember that awful day when Poppa threw everything out the window and burned it.

"Maybe it's because the *attic* is where he hid the missing piece of his heart." But, if that were true, Daniel thought, then Poppa didn't bury his heart in the coffin with Momma after all. "That means the piece of his heart isn't gone forever. . . ."

"And it means," she said conspiratorially, "that we can get it back."

This was the first good news in months, and it brought smiles to both their faces. All that was left to do was to get Poppa up to the attic.

Their plan, however, would have to wait because the next morning something awful happened.

CHAPTER 11

The next morning

At half past seven in the morning, a stranger knocked on their kitchen door. He introduced himself to Joseph as Charlie Mulch, president of the bank—the very bank that held the note for the Hutchinson farm. He was dressed in a black, heavy wool overcoat. Around the stranger the air was frigid, and behind him the skies were overcast.

Joseph ordered his children out of the kitchen. The children went into the front room where they could hear and occasionally sneak a peek.

Joseph sat at the opposite end of the kitchen table from Mr. Mulch. He did not offer him anything warm to drink like Miriam would have.

Mr. Mulch explained the bank's position for a good ten minutes. Joseph was dumbfounded. He pushed away from the table, and then he walked across the room saying he was confused and that he did not understand. He raised his voice, exclaiming, "I cannot believe you are doing this."

"Calm down," the bank president told him. "Take a seat."

"But how is it possible?" Joseph exclaimed.

"You're taking it personally, Mr. Hutchinson," the president said nervously, as if trying to stick to a text that had been practiced on many people before him.

"But it is personal, Mulch," Joseph exclaimed, banging his fist on the table, face flushed and perspiring. "It doesn't get any more personal than this."

"Now, now," the president repeated, forcing a smile. "Let's be calm."

Joseph could take it no longer. "You are throwing me and my family off our farm! I'll calm down when you are out of my house!"

"Mr. Hutchinson, I told you that this is just business."

Through clenched teeth, he spat out, "I want you out of my house."

Daniel and Mary gasped.

"Don't you understand that the bank is in business to do business?"

"To kick a man when he is down—you call that business? My family has paid you what we owed you steady as rain."

Even as he spoke the words, Joseph knew they were a lie. He had missed payments to the bank since the children were born; a fact so shameful he had kept it hidden even from Miriam. Only now did Joseph realize the gravity of his situation. He lashed out, "For God sakes, man, my wife just died."

The tension was unbearable to Charlie Mulch. "I'm truly sorry for your loss," he said, turning away from Joseph and walking to the door to let himself out. "But a deal's a deal. You were the one who defaulted, Mr. Hutchinson," spilled from Mulch's lips in such an accusatory tone that one would have thought that Joseph had just robbed the bank.

The children understood this much—Poppa had done something wrong.

"Wait, Mr. Mulch," Joseph cried out abruptly. "If I could give you a little money now—" he stumbled toward the sideboard where their money was kept, "with a promise of more to come. . . ." But his voice trailed off as he opened the drawer. The bit of money they had now rested in the pocket of the doctor who could not save Miriam's life. "Never mind," Joseph muttered as he closed the empty drawer.

If you looked closely you could see it happen—like when a pin pricks the surface of the skin and blood slowly spills out—what was left of Joseph's life force seeped out of him until he no longer had the strength to stand on his own two feet. He sat down as if he might never again get up.

Mulch's message was clear: Joseph had until the end of November to vacate the farm that had been in his family for generations.

The meeting was over. Mr. Mulch turned to go, but not before seeing Daniel and Mary peeking around the corner at him. He wished he had not seen them staring at him with their big, terrified eyes; it would have made his job easier. He walked out the door without a goodbye, but no longer with a clear conscience.

The children looked at each other, faces white with fear. The thought of asking Poppa to go up to the attic was, at the moment, absolutely out of the question.

CHAPTER 12

Two days later

While the children were busily packing up their few clothes from the storage cubby, Joseph finally made it up to the attic to retrieve the Hutchinson Bible.

He climbed the two flights of stairs; what else was there to do but put one foot in front of the other and salvage what was left of his family? He unlocked the attic door, swung it open, and stepped inside the cold, empty room. The single window, violently broken, then hastily boarded up, blocked out the sun's light and warmth. He walked the few steps to the single chair and sank down onto it, weary beneath the weight of sorrow and regret. *What good is a father who can't provide food and shelter for his children?* The thought was like a fist hammering down on him.

"You're a fool," he said aloud, "to have put all your faith in this room." He had learned a hard lesson.

He sat for a while and soon his breathing calmed, and his bitter thoughts quieted. He adjusted his eyes to the dim light in this place he once considered sacred and took one last look around. With nothing in the way he could finally see the attic for what it was: wide plank floors in need of washing, rough, bare walls, the window he hastily boarded up with left-over planks from the barn. Joseph couldn't help but smile—it was his worst carpentry job ever!

As he stared at the window something struck him as very odd. Why was the wall beneath the window the only wall finished? He rose to his feet with the curiosity of a cat and approached the wall slowly. He kneeled down and ran his hand along the surface of the wood. Upon closer examination, he felt a loose board beneath the palm of his hand and excitedly pried it off. What Joseph saw behind the wall stunned him.

CHAPTER 13

Moments later

❧ The two tiny hands tugging at his sleeve came as a complete surprise to Joseph.

"What do you see in there, Poppa?" Mary asked.

Joseph turned towards them and looked at his two beautiful children. Goodness knows, he hadn't really seen them in months.

Daniel and Mary stood perfectly still. Oh, it felt so good to be seen by him.

Daniel could stand there forever; however, there was a limit to Mary's six-year-old patience. She had to ask. "Poppa, did you find the missing piece of your heart behind that wall?"

Overcome with love, all he could do was hug them.

Mary had to know. "Did you, Poppa?"

"I don't know what's behind the wall, Mary, but I need your help to find out. So wait here while I get a lamp so we can see what we are doing." With that Joseph ran down the stairs.

When he returned, he set them to work. "You two start breaking off the wood, and I'll help you."

And so they began to work together as a family. They were being pushed off their farm, had nowhere to go, did not know what to do next, but in this moment, they were as happy as they'd ever been. Joseph showed them the best way to dislodge the panels of wood. The children followed Joseph's lead by kicking with their feet what they couldn't break with their hands. Soon their shirts were plastered to their backs and their hair to their foreheads; they grunted and groaned and suffered in silence the pinpricks of one-too-many splinters. The space was cold and, to Joseph's knowledge, had never been properly swept or dusted, which ex-plained Daniel's sneezing and Mary's runny nose. Yet no one stopped, nor complained, nor gave up until the entire wall was re-moved.

"What is it?" Daniel whispered, wide-eyed.

Joseph pulled it out of hiding and laid it

on the floor. "It's a chest of some sort." But it was like no chest he had ever seen before . . . or was it?

Joseph figured that it was about seven inches wide by five inches high and maybe seven inches deep. It seemed so decrepit that one strong wind might collapse the small structure. The paper-thin, dirt-encrusted strips of wood were braced by four tarnished brass hinges that appeared to have more character than strength. And when Joseph carefully manipulated the little lock, it broke apart. On the top of what might have once been a mahogany chest was a slit into which you could slip things.

"Maybe it's a bank," Mary ventured, biting her nails in an agony of suspense.

Maybe, they all thought. It was as good a guess as any. But nothing could have been further from the truth.

Mary really did try to control herself but she could not—she grabbed for the lid of the chest and clumsily flung it open. When the lid fell back on its hinges, the entire chest collapsed. There in the center of what was once a chest lay a very, very old, water-stained, four-by-six-inch plain brown notebook resting atop a pile of ancient slips of paper.

They stared speechlessly at the note-book.

Daniel and Mary knew that this mystery was better than any they'd told each other at night under the covers, because this one was real.

Joseph suggested they continue down-stairs. He handed Daniel the remains of the chest. To Mary he entrusted the notebook but told her not to open it until he arrived. He collected the pile of tiny folded slips of paper—but the few words written upon each were so faint only a few stray letters remained legible.

CHAPTER 14

A few minutes later

Daniel laid the remains of the chest on the kitchen table with great care. Mary placed the ancient notebook beside it. Joseph's last instructions were clear—they had to wait for him.

But much as they wanted to obey his wishes, they found they could not leave the notebook alone. It had cast an intoxicating spell over them so much so that when Joseph poured them each a cup of milk, it was all they could do not to grab the notebook while his back was turned. Who could say whether the children just needed some magic in their lives or if this chest and notebook possessed real power?

"Poppa, you were the one who found the book in the box," Daniel announced, taking charge, "so you should be the one to read it."

Mary had her heart set on reading from

the special book until she remembered she could hardly read.

The children looked expectantly towards Joseph. Joseph lifted the old-fashioned notebook and placed it in the palm of his hand. It weighed no more than a handful of feathers. He flipped open the cover and began reading the first page.

Bring your prayers
to the Prayer Chest, my son,
and all that you ask
shall be answered one by one.

"The box is a prayer chest, Poppa," Mary cried. "A chest of prayers."

"Not quite, sweetheart," he answered. "It seems to be a chest *for* prayers." That explained the opening at the top of the chest and the mysterious slips of paper within. "It says that if you put your prayers into the chest they will be answered—"

"All of them?" Mary interrupted.

"All that you ask shall be answered one by one," Joseph recited, relieved that the notebook was nothing more than a fairy tale.

Apparently Daniel thought otherwise and

released a long, low whistle at the magnitude of their find.

Joseph read on,

THE SECRET OF THE PRAYER CHEST

WRITTEN ON 26 OF MARCH 1780, EASTER MORNING, BY MALACHI HUTCHINSON FOR HIS NEWBORN SON, JOSEPH.

"Is that you, Poppa?" Mary asked excitedly.

Daniel groaned. They were sitting in the presence of a genuine treasure, and Mary was asking one stupid question after another. Fearing some lengthy explanation by Joseph, Daniel jumped in hastily and explained that more than one person could have the same name, and the same birthday for that matter. "Please, Poppa," he pressed, "turn the page."

I write this to help you, Joseph my son, for you are about to be born into a world that is not perfect, a world often hard and confusing, a world

*where nearly all prayers go
unanswered.*

*I am twenty-three years old, making
me thus far the oldest living Hutchinson
man. You may ask how can a man so
young have wisdom enough to be of
assistance to you. To which I say, living
in the shadow of death each day gives
even an ordinary man uncommon
wisdom. This is why Grandmother Mary
passed down the secret to me that I am
about to pass on to you.*

"Grandma Mary?" Mary exclaimed with
glee. "She has my name, Poppa. We both
have the very same name."

"Here we go again," Daniel moaned dramatically. "Please, Poppa," he implored.

"Hush, Mary, Daniel's right. Let's do the
reading first, and then we'll get to your
questions." Joseph continued reading,

*What secret could a plain chest
contain that would necessitate it being
passed down to each generation since
as far back as any Hutchinson can
remember?*

*My son, the secret of the Prayer
Chest is the greatest secret of all time.
It is the secret of new life.*

*This is why I waited to write you
until Easter morning. The Prayer Chest
fulfills the secret promise made on that
day. The Prayer Chest you hold in your
hands is the doorway through which
heaven enters and reveals itself on
earth in your life.*

Joseph lifted his eyes from the notebook.
In the black reflection of the glass window
panes flashed the face of the angel who had
said, "I have come to take something from
you and give you something far greater in
return." In her hands she had been holding
this very chest. A hundred distinct thoughts,
as individual as snowflakes, vied for his attention.

The children threatened to seize control
of the book if he stopped reading, so
Joseph read on,

*Trust that there is nothing more
important in your life at this moment
than to learn the secret of the Prayer
Chest. Nothing.*

If you turn out to be as skeptical a man as I once was, Joseph, then you shall understand the question I put to Grandma Mary. Is learning the secret more important than putting out a fire in my home, Grandma?

"*Especially if you are putting out a fire,*" *she answered.*

I can only repeat to you what Grandma Mary told me, so I cannot tell you why it works, only that it does.

Malachi's newborn son, Joseph, might have been the intended recipient, but he could not have needed these words more than Joseph, who was busy putting out fires of his own.

Be certain, my son, before you turn to the next page that you are ready.

Joseph looked up from the page. "Are we ready?"

"Absolutely!"

He wished that he were that certain. Joseph had a month to figure out how to feed his family and under what roof he was

going to shelter them. "It's bedtime," he announced, not knowing what else to do.

Very reluctantly the children agreed to go
to bed, under the condition that at sunup
they'd meet back at the table and continue
reading from the mysterious notebook.
Joseph promised, but it took all his will-
power not to slip the notebook in his back
pocket as they climbed the stairs to their
bedrooms.

CHAPTER 15

The next morning

The next morning Joseph descended the stairs to find his children at the table awaiting the next installment. He couldn't remember a single time when they had preceded him in breaking their morning fast. The milk was poured, the panbread buttered, and a crackling fire beckoned from the hearth. In the center of the table the notebook sat untouched; his children's restraint was impressive.

Joseph took a seat at the head of the table. "A toast," he said, lifting his tumbler of milk, "to your great-great-great-great-grandfather Malachi." Joseph could only guess at the correct number of greats and clearly, at this time of the morning, the children were not keeping count. Daniel and Mary giggled in response and, despite himself, he found their excitement infectious. Outwardly he laughed along with his children, but inwardly he worried that he might be perceived as a laughingstock: with the sky falling down around him, he who swore he would never again put his faith in anything was putting his faith in some ancient, broken chest that made impossible promises it could not possibly keep.

Joseph could not explain what drew him forward, he could only follow. He opened the book and began to read,

> *I introduce you to The Secret of the Prayer Chest in the way that Grandma Mary did me—through questions that invite reason rather than response, my son.*
>
> *Grandma Mary began thusly:*
>
> *"Since the beginning of time every man and woman has prayed— hundreds upon thousands of prayers daily. Why then are only a handful of them answered?*
>
> *"Is it a person's goodness that determines it, or his piety? Perhaps his cleverness or his generosity to the old and infirm? If it is goodness that determines it, why are the prayers of unkind and selfish men answered?*

"*Even the deepest thinkers have not found the final piece to the puzzle of prayer—why some prayers were answered and others not—and this, as you can imagine, weighed heavily on the mind of man.*"

Stone-by-stone, dear Joseph, Grandma Mary laid the foundation of her argument.

"*After living in the mystery of unanswered prayers, generation after generation, it proved to be an unbearable frustration to mankind. Man wanted peace of mind, even a false peace would be better than this frustrating and fruitless pursuit.*

"*Here then, Malachi, is what mankind agreed to believe so that the search for the elusive answer might come to an end: It is God's Will that chooses which prayers are to be answered and which are not.*"

I confessed to Grandma Mary that this was the very belief I held about prayer.

"*Look and you shall see, Malachi,*" she said with a leaden sadness, "*how this belief at once calms you, yet robs you of your capacity to have your prayers answered."*

It took me many sleepless nights to understand why Grandma Mary called this the great lie. But after much wrangling, I did understand.

"Slip one hundred prayers into the chest and do not use the secrets of the Prayer Chest and all one hundred shall go unanswered. Slip one hundred prayers into the chest using the secrets of the Prayer Chest, and every last one shall be answered—to the utmost.

"The Prayer Chest returns to mankind the authority to have our prayers answered and to use that authority as we wish."

Grandma Mary placed the Prayer Chest in my hands for emphasis.

"You hold in your hands," she said gravely, "the doorway between heaven and earth."

Admittedly, I grew anxious with the responsibility. If you feel similarly, know that there is no shame in this, my son.

*Grandma looked straight through
me as she might a pane of glass, and
said, "You must decide, Malachi, if
you want to hold such a power in
your hands. If you do, you will never
hold the Prayer Chest nor your
prayers lightly."*

*I thought long and hard about my
decision before speaking it aloud.
"Yes," I declared, "I do want to hold
the power of the Prayer Chest in my
hands."*

*What is your decision, Joseph, my
son?*

Joseph put the notebook down and
asked himself the same question. Somehow he felt that his answer might be of real
importance in his life.

He turned to Daniel and Mary and said,
"You two will each have to decide for your-
selves."

*If you decide to accept the power
that comes with the Prayer Chest, my
son, then I shall without delay pass
down the First Secret of Prayer that
Grandma Mary shared with me.*

Maybe it took almost losing everything before Joseph could yield to the Prayer Chest without so much as a second thought. "I've decided," he announced, inviting the children to do the same.

"Yesyesyesyes," their words tumbled out, one atop the other, sounding like one long affirmation. Between them they did not have a single doubt.

The notebook was written in an old-fashioned block-style script. The quill pen Malachi used leaked here and there, but the text was legible. Each page was punctuated with small illustrations highlighting important points for emphasis. Joseph put the book into Daniel's hands. "I'll read along with you, Daniel."

Daniel was overwhelmed—Joseph had never asked him to read aloud before. He cleared his throat and read carefully,

THE FIRST SECRET OF THE PRAYER CHEST:
PRAYER IS ANSWERED THROUGH YOU.

Daniel could read it but could not quite understand it. What good was having a secret if he did not know what it meant? He turned to Joseph.

"Don't ask me without giving it some thought, Daniel," Joseph replied, not quite understanding it himself. "What do you think it means?"

Daniel spoke tentatively. "Does it mean . . . if I pray for something . . . I have to let that thing happen to me first?" When Joseph didn't stop him, he forged on, "The Prayer Chest is like a door—"

"And you have to open the door." Mary was pleased to have found a piece of the puzzle by herself.

"And when we open it," Daniel continued, "our answer comes in?"

Clearly none of this had anything to do with paying off the money he owed to the bank, but Joseph let his children lose themselves in the mystery. "The answer to our prayer comes in through the open door of the Prayer Chest and through the open door in your chest where your heart is," he explained with a wisdom that surprised him.

"Then what's the answer to our prayer?" Daniel asked. "Us opening the door or us getting what we want?"

"Both. What we want and what heaven wants for us are answered the moment that we open the door to our heart."

It was as if an innate faith long buried in Joseph emerged and spoke through him. The faith of Grandma Mary.

In her own way, Mary understood it, too. "If I pray for something good to happen, Poppa, then I have to let it come through my heart first."

When did his children get so wise, Joseph wondered, looking back over the storm of suffering they had all weathered since Miriam's passing.

"I got it," Daniel exploded. "I know what my prayer is."

"Then write it down, Daniel, and slip it into the Prayer Ch—" Joseph stopped abruptly. As they all looked at the remains of the chest, they laughed aloud for the first time in months.

"Can you make us a new Prayer Chest, Poppa?" Daniel pleaded, meaning now, right now.

More than anything, Joseph wanted to be a good father, but he was uncertain if that meant packing up possessions and planning for his family's future, or spending the day in the barn building a Prayer Chest.

"The bank man said we don't have to be out of the house until the end of November," Daniel explained. "It shouldn't take that long for our prayers to be answered."

Daniel's certainty was the deciding factor. "You have your mother's faith," Joseph said. They bundled themselves up in mismatched layers of clothing and headed toward the barn.

A small pile of siding left over from the construction of Miriam's coffin was stacked up in the center of the barn. They sat down on stools facing the pile. "If you are very quiet, you will hear the wood whisper," Joseph said to them, as Grandpa Elijah had once said to him. Of course, he knew the wood did not whisper any more than the crops did. But in the same way a farmer connects with the cycles of his land and can almost hear his crops growing, that is the way Grandpa Elijah wanted him to be with the wood—so connected that he was one with it.

The children were shivering in the drafty barn listening to the wood as hard as they could. They wanted to hear the wood whisper to them for their father's sake. Sadly, however, they heard nothing beyond the chattering of their miserably cold teeth.

Finally, Joseph realized that the Prayer Chest should be made out of the wood from the attic and the remains of Malachi's chest, not the barn siding.

For the better part of the next hour the children traveled back and forth from the farmhouse to the barn.

When they were done, the three Hutchinsons sat before the small pile of wood with anticipation, as if the pieces might jump up and begin assembling themselves. They waited and watched and waited some more until Joseph began sharing his plans for construction of the Prayer Chest.

"I'm going to make the chest the same size as Malachi's. We can support the four corners with the elbow hinges from the original chest. You two will have to clean the dirt and polish them the best you can." The children wanted the chest, not a detailed work order explaining how to construct one.

Mary convinced Joseph to let them return to the warm house to write their prayers.

After eating, then thinking, then napping,

then writing, the children compared their prayers. A great discussion ensued: Which one of them would read their prayer first? What if they prayed for the wrong thing? What if they prayed for opposite things— would the prayers cancel each other out?

When all the issues were resolved, each submitted a prayer for the other's scrutiny. On separate sheets of paper, in separate handwriting, was the same prayer.

Make Poppa happy.

CHAPTER 16

Several hours later

Joseph completed the project. He walked round and round the chest examining it from every angle, feeling every inch of its surface. He should have been satisfied when the wood beneath his hands felt as smooth as silk, but still he was not. Something important was missing. He held the chest in his hands and silently, just as Grandpa Elijah might have done, Joseph asked to be shown what was missing. It wasn't long before he saw it in his mind's eye—the angel's chest was fastened by a tiny lock that shone brightly, a lock made of pure gold.

Pure gold. Well, thought Joseph sarcastically, why not line the inside of the chest with rubies, or better yet, diamonds? Where would the money come from for such an extravagance? He dismissed the possibility as fantastical.

Tucking the wooden chest under his arm, he made his way back to the farmhouse where his children awaited. He swung open the door and called out, "It's finished."

It was Joseph's simplest carpentry job and yet his greatest work of art. With the exception of Miriam's coffin, he had built nothing with more reverence than this. The wood of this Prayer Chest was infused with the fullness of his heart's unspoken dreams for his family.

Joseph laid the chest in the center of the table and saw Daniel's and Mary's eyes widen with wonder. He saw the paper and quill pen and ink the children left for him to write down his prayer.

He sat down and took the pen in his hand. His prayer was all he'd thought about as he built the chest. It was what he wanted more than anything in the world. Joseph dipped the pen, tapped off the excess ink and carefully wrote his prayer.

Please take care of my children.

He wiped a tear from the corner of his eye before it fell, hoping the children had not noticed.

They noticed.

Before he permitted them to slip their

prayers into the chest, Joseph said, "If we are going to do this, let's do it right." Then he read aloud the three remaining sentences of the First Secret from the notebook,

Write your prayer and place it in the Prayer Chest. Do not remove or amend your prayer for any reason at any future time. Do not unlock the Chest.

"The lock, Poppa. The lock is missing!" the children cried out.

Joseph explained that it wasn't missing, but that they did not have the money to buy the kind of lock that the Prayer Chest needed, a lock made of pure gold. He told them that he was hoping the chest would work as well without one. They all agreed to pretend there was a lock on the chest and to never open it.

"I hope maybe someday we will be able to afford such a lock," Joseph said wistfully.

"It will come, Poppa," Daniel said, as if he knew it for a fact. "You will see."

Joseph folded over the sheet of paper with his prayer on it and slipped it into the opening at the top of the chest. After folding her sheet of paper as many times as it would fold, Mary followed suit. Daniel kissed the paper with his prayer on it before dropping it into the chest.

There was no way they could have known that miles away, the answers to their prayers had already begun to take form.

CHAPTER 17

The next morning

Charlie Mulch awoke with a splitting headache. Not a man to suffer in silence, he woke up his wife to comfort him.

Daisy rubbed his shoulders, put cold cloths on his forehead, and gave him some extra love. Charlie was a good man. He was also as stubborn as a knot, but she alone knew that beneath his steely exterior beat a soft heart; this discrepancy was the cause of his headaches.

When the pain got the better of him, Charlie would serve her up the same old excuses. "If I am weak, everyone in the bank will take advantage of me." Or, "The bank is a battlefield," he'd say, when Daisy called him a bully. Why should she argue when Charlie's headaches were the better teacher?

"Business is not about having people love you, Daisy."

In this arena Charlie excelled, for other than Daisy, he did not have a single friend in the world. Even his colleagues at the bank did not care for the way Charlie pushed people around in the process of doing his job.

To the young employees sent to him for training, Charlie challenged, "Soft or hard, pick one," he'd say with his finger making its blunt point in their chest. "If you're weak, the next man will walk over you, but strong, you will walk over him."

Neither choice appealed but his trainees knew what Mr. Mulch wanted to hear. Over time many a promising young employee left the bank to pursue another line of work, one with heart. Sure the business world was hard, they thought, but it didn't have to be this hard. Charlie thought it did.

Daisy married the man beneath the official façade, the man who let his guard down only when he thought no one was looking. Tenderly she asked, "What is troubling you, Husband?"

"I had a job to do, and I can't make peace with it."

"What did you do, dear?"

Charlie closed his eyes; it would be easier to admit if he did not have to look at her. "I had to foreclose on a man's farm."

"What happened? Surely *something* must have happened to his family."

"I'm the president of the bank, not his best friend. In fact, he's been missing payments for years. He left me no choice."

"Charlie," she began kindly, "what did the farmer say?"

Charlie focused on his fingers, the cotton patchwork quilt, the twittering birds outside his window, anything but Daisy.

Daisy massaged his temples and waited. Sooner or later his guilt would lead him to confess it.

"He said his wife was—" his voice lowering a notch with each syllable, "ill." Rolling thunder throbbed at the base of his skull.

"How ill, Charlie?"

Had she asked him to lift a bank vault upon his shoulders, it would have been easier than answering this question. Like an echo rising up from the depths of an invisible valley, he said, "She died."

Daisy did not attempt to disguise her exasperation. "Oh, my hard-headed, soft-hearted man, what am I going to do with you?" She embraced him, laying his head upon her shoulder. "What's his name, dear, and I'll see if there's anything I can do to help." She could help them pack, bring them food, watch the children. Daisy did not have to ask; she knew there were children.

"Hutchinson."

Daisy sat up straight. "Charlie, please tell me that it's not Joseph Hutchinson."

"Yes. It is. Why?"

"Darling! Don't you remember who his grandfather was?" she asked, even though it was apparent by his silence that he didn't. "It was David Hutchinson that saved my Grandpa Edward's life—"

"When they were hunting together as young boys!" Charlie chimed in, relieved to remember.

Was there anyone in the county who had not heard this story? Grandpa Edward was kicked by a frightened buck, and David carried him in his arms for four miles into town. The doctor said that if David hadn't come to the rescue, her grandpa would have died from the bleeding in his belly.

"We owe the Hutchinsons, Charlie." Daisy did not need to be told what the right thing to do was—she knew it in her heart. "First thing tomorrow morning, I am going to the

Hutchinsons to help them figure out a way to stay on their farm."

Charlie looked mortified.

"And you are going with me."

CHAPTER 18

Later that night

The Prayer Chest sat facing them with the unopened notebook by its side. The day had held one surprise after another for Daniel and Mary, but the best was yet to come: The Second Secret of the Prayer Chest. They drummed their fingers in anticipation and tapped their feet on the scuffed oak floorboards, but it did not make Joseph come any faster. He was in his bedroom with the door closed, and they knew better than to disturb him.

Joseph sat on the edge of his bed in silence. His calloused hands clutched the quilt as if to squeeze the life out of it at the thought of not being able to provide for his children.

Bring your prayers
to the Prayer Chest, my son, . . .

If only he could have talked it out with the president of the bank. If the man had been willing to work with him, or help him, or just listen. Joseph was sure that together they could have worked something out.

If only his father and brothers had not been Hutchinsons and died so young—they might all be alive today, laboring together, supporting one another. And when Joseph came to them with a problem, they would have helped him to resolve it. He would not have had to figure his life out all by himself or turn to a stupid box for help.

If only his mother had not made him promise to keep the farm in the family when she passed, he would have been free to move on, to work at what he loved most in the world, to spend his days covered in sawdust.

and all that you ask
shall be answered one by one.

With Miriam gone, there was no one left to talk to, to lean on. Everyone left in his family leaned on him. He realized anew how strong Miriam had been, how much she had helped him. Would she ever forgive him? Would he ever forgive himself?

He opened his mouth, wanting to speak his prayer aloud, *take care of my children,* but no words came out. The few tiny seeds of faith that had begun to take root in his heart had been crushed under the heel of reality.

Is learning the secret more important than putting out a fire in my home? . . . Especially if you are putting out a fire.

He lowered his head into his hands, his eyes wet with tears, and sat for a good quarter of an hour on the edge of the abyss that was his family's future.

When Joseph came down the stairs, Daniel and Mary smiled. But when he took his seat and opened the notebook without a wink or a warm word, the children felt his sadness, his despair.

Oh, they wished they could rush to him and hug him so hard and tell him everything would be all right, but they did no such thing. Everything was not all right, and they knew it. Momma was gone and soon their farm and their home would be gone. Poppa's misery made its way into their young hearts like a gray smoke that slips through cracks and under closed doors. Inevitably their sadness turned to fear. What would become of them? Like the siren's song calling sailors to their death, the voice of fear frightened them but they could not stop listening. Tears made their silent way down the children's cheeks. Their father was too big to cry, but the children knew that his tears were spilling over on the inside.

In time, Joseph reached for the notebook and flipped it open. He read,

THE SECOND SECRET OF THE PRAYER CHEST: PRAYER IS ANSWERED WHEN YOU LISTEN.

When you talk you are a dam overflowing, but when you listen you are an open vessel ready to receive.

Reluctantly I disclose to you that I was such a man whose words spilled over. Like a drum I banged my prayer into God's head in an effort to help God remember.

The Second Secret means write your prayer down once and talk no more of

it to God. From that point forth listen. Only listen.

"And where," I asked Grandma Mary, "might a farmer like me with chores to do from sunrise to sundown find time to listen?"

"Return to your work, do what you must, but with a part of you ever inclined toward listening. Know that God speaks to us continuously, but we cannot hear if we do not listen."

That God must work so hard to get our attention wrenches my heart, my son.

Joseph turned the page intending to read the third secret, but the text cautioned him otherwise.

Do not read the Third Secret until you have spent this night listening. You will be surprised by how much one is able to hear in the silence.

Joseph closed the notebook and pushed it across the table. Without a single word of protest, they rose and climbed the stairs to their bedrooms.

Tonight the prayer in all three of their hearts was simple: they prayed for sleep, where a sweet, albeit temporary, forgetfulness awaited them.

CHAPTER 19

Early the next morning

Joseph, Daniel, and Mary were following Grandma Mary's advice to the letter—listening as they packed up the very small collection of kitchen utensils in crates. Surprisingly, when measured in wooden crates, their life without Momma did not amount to much.

In the midst of their packing and listening, the unexpected knocking at the door startled them. Daniel opened the door to a bad dream: the man from the bank was standing on their porch with a lady. A trace of resentment stole across his face, but he bit down the words that matched the feeling. "Wait here," he warned. "I'll get my Poppa." That was as nice as he could manage to be.

Joseph traded places with Daniel at the door. Without hesitation, he welcomed the couple with the kind of warmth you might get from a pen-and-ink drawing of a sun. He motioned to his antagonists to have a seat at the table.

Listen to what the man has to say, he told himself, turning his back on them to set the water boiling for tea. There was an iron taste in his mouth when he apologized for having no sweets or breads to accompany the tea.

"Oh, that won't be necessary, Mr. Hutchinson," Daisy said kindly.

Meet badness with goodness, Miriam would often counsel him when she sensed his disposition darken. Her voice was as close as his breath. "How can I help you? As you can see we're in the middle of packing," Joseph said harshly. He took a seat. The children flanked him on either side in the event that they had to protect him.

Daisy placed her hand on Charlie's wrist as their private signal for him to begin.

"My wife Daisy here told me an interesting story about your Grandfather David, Mr. Hutchinson. I wonder if your ears were ringing yesterday morning when we spoke of him. It seems that when your grandfather was a boy he saved Daisy's grandfather's life."

Joseph was a locked gate.

Daisy used the opportunity to connect

with the children, telling them the charmingly embellished version of their great-grandfather's heroics. "He was a strong and brave boy," she began.

Though on their guard, Mary and Daniel warmed to Daisy. They were hungry for such tender-hearted attention.

"Did you know," she said leaning in toward them, "that when our grandfathers were boys, they were the very, very best of friends?"

"When I told Daisy that you were a Hutchinson," Charlie jumped in, "she said that we had to do something to stop you from being put off your farm. That's why we are here . . . to help you . . . and to say I'm sorry for the way I treated you," he stammered. "And I mean that, Mr. Hutchinson."

"You are here to *help* me keep the farm?" Joseph asked in disbelief.

All Hutchinson eyes turned toward the Prayer Chest.

That is what made Charlie notice it, too, resting conspicuously in the center of the kitchen table. "What a handsome box," he said, genuinely admiring the craftsmanship.

"Thank you, Mr. Mulch," Joseph said

mechanically, unsure of what to make of this turn of events.

"Call me Charlie, please." He extended his hand and enthusiastically pumped Joseph's hand with the kind of relief a guilty man feels upon being forgiven.

The bubbling hum of the boiling water signaled intermission.

Joseph left the table to tend to the tea, suppressing the urge to grab his children and spin them around the room.

"Who made this chest?" Charlie inquired.

"Poppa made it," Mary said. "Poppa made everything in the house that is made of wood. Which is just about everything."

"May I examine the box?"

"Only if you don't open it," Daniel cautioned. "There are very personal things inside."

"I respect your right to privacy, son, thank you for telling me." Charlie picked up the box and, with excessive care to keep it closed, appreciated its utter simplicity. Unlike other men, he understood that the simpler a chest appears the more expert the craftsmanship; so simple was this chest that it led you to believe that you could build one like it yourself if you had a mind to, only to find that it was nearly impossible.

"Are you a carpenter?" Charlie asked with admiration.

"It's just a hobby," Joseph deflected, still not sure where this talk was leading.

"This table," Charlie surveyed, "and the chairs and the bureau—you built them?"

"Yes," he answered humbly. "Sooner or later everything needed replacing."

"Although my wife won't admit it, Joseph, I'm a rotten carpenter—"

"Oh, I admit it, dear, just not while you are in the room," Daisy laughed easily.

"I've been talking about adding on to our home for years—an office for me and a sewing room and maybe two bedrooms for Daisy's relatives. You seem to have a natural talent for it, Mr. Hutchinson," he said turning the box over in his hands. Charlie could not get over how handsome the chest was. He wondered if Joseph would make him one like it.

Daisy could've hugged her husband for this inspired idea. "What Charlie is trying to say, Mr. Hutchinson," she improvised, "is that we would be grateful if you considered coming to work for us. This is not a favor, mind you. We need your help and, of course, we would make it well worth your while financially."

Charlie let his wife set Joseph's pay. She was better able to calculate the full cost of the man's labor and the additional fee for Charlie's guilt.

"In this way, Mr. Hutchinson, you can remain on your farm," Daisy explained, "and afford to make your payments to the bank."

This is what they agreed to: the following Monday Joseph was to begin work on the Mulch home. The carriage was to pick him up at the Brown farm at seven in the morning. He knew that Grace would be more than willing to tend to his children.

Joseph stood up tall and spoke this quietly, "Thank you both." In the privacy of his heart he felt a glimmer of hope.

Though her heart was full from spending time with the Hutchinsons, on the carriage ride home Daisy nonetheless began to grow despondent. Her life was not unlike riding in this carriage, sitting with her back to the horses, seeing only where she had been and not where she was heading. Who knew what was going to happen next? Daisy did not like surprises. Her biggest surprise, her childlessness, still caused her pain. She daydreamed about embracing Daniel in her arms and rocking Mary to sleep at night as if they were her very own babies.

Charlie had a daydream of his own—he wondered if Joseph would make him a chest of his own. From the instant he lifted the chest in his hands, Charlie had a queer, restless feeling that he could not name. In a hidden chamber of his heart where the authentic Charlie Mulch dwelled, a lock unfastened and a door opened, allowing him to see with unmistakable clarity what his headaches had been trying to teach him, that hiding was no safer than outright exposure.

Hours later, at their evening meal, when Daisy asked him what had given him the idea to hire Joseph, Charlie told her it was as if the chest had spoken to him and had told him to do so.

CHAPTER 20

Two days later

When Grace suggested feeding his family, Joseph surprised her by accepting. He had been as self-sufficient as a stone these last three months, but not today. Friday at exactly twelve noon, the Hutchinsons arrived. Grace and her daughter Rose were still in the kitchen creating the meal in honor of Joseph's good news. When finally they emerged with tray after overflowing tray of food, Joseph understood the delay. Grace had not prepared a meal but a feast. The food was so plentiful there was hardly table space remaining for the five water-filled tumblers.

Grace's voice sang out, "Come Hutchinsons. Come and let the Brown women feed you." Rose's back straightened with pride as she heard herself addressed as a woman.

Daniel and Mary raced one another to get their seats on either side of Joseph, but

Joseph was in no hurry to get anywhere. For once, life was coming to him—Monday a carriage was coming to transport him into his dream of being a carpenter.

Grace was seated at the head of the oval table observing the merry sight. As a family of two, she and Rose had selfishly cherished their intimate solitude above all else. Until now. She basked in the noisy cheerfulness and gaiety that was part of a large family. A large family, what a marvelous thought.

After grace was recited, the amens said, and the food dished out, Daniel announced to Rose, "Your home is too girlie for me."

"Then it's a good thing that you don't live here," Rose countered.

"Don't listen to him." Mary added, "I think your house looks beautiful."

Everyone joined in the laughter because it was true. Where the Hutchinson home was furnished to be functional, the Brown home was designed with an eye toward comfort and beauty. It was obvious that no man had lived in this house since Grace's husband left her: frilly starched white curtains and peach slip-covered couches, dozens of lovely wall hangings with multicolored ribbons and sashes hanging from them, and silk-covered pastel pillows resting upon all available seats and surfaces. Sumptuous, inviting, and, Daniel was right, girlie.

They ate and ate until the two roast chickens were reduced to skeletons, and the breads, biscuits, and puddings a mere memory. The three children waited for the nod of approval to leave the table. Daniel, Mary, and Joseph shared a clandestine glance to confirm their silent agreement—not to speak of the Prayer Chest.

When the children left the room, Grace let her mind wander unsupervised. She, who never gave a thought to living the rest of her life without a man, was giving it a thought now. She felt silly, and she felt guilty, so she got busy clearing the table.

Joseph's dream was within reach. "Monday is two days away, Grace."

Grace smiled at him from across the room but kept moving.

"Working the farm has been like carrying a sack of rocks on my back everyday from one end of my land to another." Joseph heaved a monumental sigh of relief. "Come Monday I can finally put that burden down."

"Joseph Hutchinson, Carpenter," Grace

announced from the kitchen. "Choose a job you love," Grace recited, balancing plates and platters in her folded arms, "and you will never have to work a day in your life."

"You are a good friend, Gracie, and have always been a good teacher to me."

"Joe, stop it," she blushed.

"I am serious. Who do you think taught me how to hire men to work my farm? You'll be proud of me because I have let the neighbors know that I'll be leasing all but five acres of my land to the highest bidder."

"You did not learn that from me," Grace protested, returning the plates to the table. "A farmer never lets go of his land, Joe."

"I am not letting it go. I am loaning it out to men who want to work it. Men who love working it, not hate it as I have."

Who was she to judge? Grace never worked a single acre of her land herself. She was a pampered only child, and when her parents died and left her the farm, she was a pampered adult. Then when she realized her husband would be of no earthly use, she cleverly decided to hire boys who needed the extra money to work her land. They worked their hearts out for those few coins, Joe among them. A man couldn't feed his family with what she paid, but a boy could buy a whole dream with them. Word of her need for planting and harvesting of her crops spread through the town and from that day to this, Grace never lacked for help, nor the boys for extra pocket change.

Joseph smiled. "With the five acres I've got left, I want to triple the size of the barn so that I can do my woodworking in it during the winter months. Plus there'll be plenty of room for Daniel to learn to ride Eleanor until the day I buy him a horse of his own. And maybe," he added, letting himself get carried away, "you and Rose can . . ." What was he saying? Joseph quickly excused himself and left the table, and the room.

When Grace was a girl, she had a terrier who acted like this; rather than sharing a prized bone or showing it off, he buried it in the earth for safe keeping.

From the other room, Joseph could breathe a bit easier. The pen and ink renderings that covered the walls caught his attention. Each piece was framed simply in wrought-iron, each a perfect rendering of life on the farm. All bore the same title, "The Good Land," but none were signed with the name of the artist. "Who drew these?" he called out to her.

Feigning ignorance, Grace said that she did not know.

Her modesty touched him, deeply. Joseph went to the kitchen and stood beside her. He spoke kindly. "You know, most women would have drowned in a sea of self-pity." He meant, of course, when her husband abandoned her.

"Oh, Joe," she replied ambiguously. Even to him she dared not admit her relief when her husband left. It was a blessing. Overnight she was free to live and work and speak as she pleased.

"He wasn't a good man," Joseph said with remarkable familiarity.

He was a brute, to be sure, having left her while she was with child, but in the end her husband left her with far more than he took from her. "I have my Rose," she replied, as if that explained everything. "Rose is my true treasure. Plus, isn't a girl allowed to make a bad decision or two in her life?"

"I never blamed you, Grace. I blamed him."

Touched by his protectiveness, she said, "What's done is done, Joe," speaking about both their lives. "What choice do we have but to move forward?"

God speaks to us continuously.

"We could do what Lot's wife did—a pillar of salt doesn't get its heart broken," Joseph offered, only half-joking.

"Turning back the hands of time is not a choice, Joe."

We cannot hear God if we do not listen.

"I think that it's a fine choice." It was the thinking behind the rock wall he built around his heart. "It sure is the safest choice."

"No, Joe, it isn't." Her lips quivered, but she would not loose the tears. Her words did not touch him, but she spoke them anyway. "Listen, Joe, our ancestors left Europe to set sail into uncharted territory. They couldn't afford to weep over what they left behind, for if they did, you and I and our beautiful children would not be here today."

How could she know that nightly, by candlelight, Joseph wrote one-page, sometimes two-page, letters to Miriam begging for forgiveness. By suggesting he let go of the past, Grace was telling him to do the impossible, to leave Miriam behind.

That God must work so hard to get our attention wrenches my heart, my son.

"Hmm . . . perhaps you are right, Grace," he said trying to placate her. "Perhaps it is time to move on," he admitted, while inwardly his mind searched for an excuse that would appease the woman. How could he expect her to understand what he had done, why he could never leave Miriam behind. "From now on, I'm going to put my needs aside and attend to my children's needs until they are grown and on their own."

It sounded to Grace like a sacrifice offered up by some long-ago saint. It was a transparent excuse.

"My past was about my happiness, and my future will be about theirs," Joseph declared, the words ringing false even to his ears.

Grace sat silently with a tight smile on her lips as Joseph worked to protect his fragile heart. The air was thick with the conversation they might have had. It was too soon to have that conversation, or perhaps it was already too late. The uncomfortable silence made her feel awkward, so Grace used the time to finish clearing the table of the dirty plates and her mind of its frivolous thoughts.

CHAPTER 21

Monday morning

Both families assembled at the Brown homestead on Monday at seven o'clock in the morning to await the Mulch carriage.

Seven o'clock came and went.

As did eight o'clock, then nine.

Daniel, Mary, and Rose walked on tiptoes, spoke in whispers, and were all but invisible.

When ten o'clock arrived with still no carriage, Joseph's faith ground to a halt. He imagined the worst—the Mulches forgot, or tricked him, or did not care what happened to the Hutchinsons after all.

He grabbed his scarf and wound it around his neck like a noose, punched his fists into the sleeves of his coat, and left the house to wrestle with his demons in private. He walked and walked through a blinding snowstorm of emotion. Joseph, like Malachi, wanted security, a certainty he could see. The answers from the Prayer Chest were leading him in the opposite direction, deeper into the unknown where there were no guarantees.

Fear, fear, fear, fear everywhere he turned. Joseph picked up a stone from the ground and hurled it at the nearest tree. Was it possible to be a Hutchinson man and not live in fear?

Suddenly the wind whipped around the bare branches of the trees, and Joseph lifted his collar against the cold. In that moment he heard a voice that was unmistakable: it was Miriam's. And she whispered, *Joseph, prayer is listening.* A shiver ran down his spine and he froze. Then he took a breath and just listened.

He listened as Miriam explained how fear made every man afraid of what tomorrow would bring, how fear could eclipse all other thoughts, and how fear could make even a strong man weak.

Miriam was right. Like lightning instantly illuminating the night sky, the truth pierced Joseph's gloom. He saw the face of his real enemy, and it wasn't the Mulches or his bad luck or his family's curse. It was fear itself.

Joseph ran straight back to Grace's home

and flew up the porch steps, threw open the front door, and told everyone to get their coats on. "I have a secret to share with you and no questions are allowed. Just follow me!"

The group crowded into the carriage and rode in anticipation to the Hutchinson farm-house, where Joseph opened the front door and motioned them inside. Without a single word of introduction, Joseph pointed to the Prayer Chest and exclaimed, "There."

Grace and Rose laid eyes on the wooden chest sitting in a lemon yellow streak of sun-light in the center of the kitchen table. "It's a box," Rose said, obviously disappointed.

"Oh, it's no ordinary box, Rose. It's called a Prayer Chest," Joseph said with rever-ence.

Grace stared at the box not knowing what to make of it. Was this Joe grasping at straws by naming it a prayer chest in hopes that it might answer his? She kept silent about her skepticism because she could see how genuinely excited he was.

"I will explain everything in a minute," Joseph promised, "but first things first. Let's start a fire and have some cider."

Rose didn't want the cider, she insisted, she just wanted the secret.

"What's your hurry?" Joseph asked, putting the cider up to heat. If anyone should be in a hurry it was him, as the deadline to vacate the farm approached. So much for the Mulch promise to keep them on their farm.

After filling everyone's mug, Joseph took his time explaining to the Browns about how they discovered the Prayer Chest in the attic, and Malachi's notebook, and the meaning of the first two secrets. When he caught them up sufficiently without overwhelming them, and answered most of Rose's questions, he opened the ancient notebook and began to read,

If you have applied the first two Secrets, you will by now have noticed your faith increasing as well as tests to your faith. Bid them both welcome, for both are signs of progress.

This is the meaning of the Third Secret, my son: from the instant you slip your prayer into the Chest, everything that comes to you is a portion of the answer to that prayer.

Joseph paused and looked up from the notebook to catch the children's mouths open in anticipation. When he caught Grace's eye, a rosy blush bloomed on her cheeks in response, and she urged him, "Please, don't stop."

Yes, it was Malachi's words, but it was Joseph who gave voice to them. He took pride in the reading of the words.

Do not make the mistake that mankind makes when it throws open its arms to growth or good fortune alone and rejects all else. Doing so leaves one lopsided, like a cart with wheels on one side only.

"We must learn from Nature, where opposites walk hand-in-hand," Grandma Mary said. "Look how effortlessly Nature shifts from day to night, season to season, releasing each in its turn."

Mankind is not like this. We choose gain over loss and light over dark, and by refusing half, we are no longer able to receive the whole of our answered prayer.

My son, make yourself ready for loss and letting go as, perhaps, part of the answer to your prayer. It may not be immediately apparent how failure leads to flourishing or loss fertilizes the ground for gain, but trust that it shall.

The Third Secret is the greatest test of our faith, and it is precisely at this point where most men fail. That is why on the precious few chance encounters that found us alone together, Grandma Mary would whisper this to me—part prayer, part advice—lest I forget, "Be like an ocean that refuses no river."

"Through an open vessel," she explained, "prayers flow unobstructed, and heaven finds an inlet and outlet through which to reveal Itself on earth." Here, then, my son, is how:

THE THIRD SECRET OF THE PRAYER CHEST: PRAYER IS ANSWERED WHEN YOU WELCOME EVERYTHING.

The Prayer Chest turned something ordinary into something extraordinary, like this everyday kitchen into a chapel. A midafternoon hush surrounded the small gathering at the table.

"Is Grandma Mary saying that bad things

are going to happen, Poppa?" Daniel asked nervously.

"Grandma's saying that change is a natural thing, not a bad thing." Joseph offered up the right words but was far from convinced himself.

"Your father is right." Grace added, "Everything changes, sweetheart." Throwing a furtive glance at Joseph, she added, "The trick is not holding on to how things used to be."

"But change is bad," Mary cried out. "Momma dying, the banker's bad visit, having to leave the farm." Grace could not be saying these changes were good.

"Some changes are hard, my dear, very hard," she said wrapping her arm around Mary. "The hardest of all is when we lose people we love."

Every one of them in their own way had suffered a loss. In the silence you could hear the crackling from the cast-iron stove.

Looking directly into Joseph's despondent eyes, Grace said, "I think life keeps changing so that we can change into the people God intended us to be." Then she slipped the notebook from Joseph's hands and reread aloud what she felt was the most important sentence.

It may not be immediately apparent how failure leads to flourishing or loss fertilizes the ground for gain, but trust that it shall.

In a whisper, Rose asked Joseph, "Can I put a prayer in the wooden box?"

Daniel, Mary, and Grace turned to Joseph.

"Of course you can, Rose, and you, too, Grace." How could something as important as the Prayer Chest not be shared?

With that, Mary ran from the room to secure paper and Poppa's quill pen and ink.

"I've had a prayer in my heart since Friday, Momma," Rose confessed. "Would you write it down for me?"

"I have to warn you Rose," Daniel advised, "the Prayer Chest works all right, but it's got to be locked for it to work all the way."

"If you put the prayer in the chest and lock it," Rose questioned, "how do you get the prayers out?"

"You don't," Mary said dramatically. "You

never take them out again for as long as you live."

"Never?" Rose asked.

"Never, ever," Mary echoed.

Grace asked Daniel why they didn't have a lock.

"Well, it's not a simple lock we are after," Joseph said, sharing a smile with the children. "We need a special kind of lock."

"I have a kitchen drawer full of locks. I will be happy to give you a half dozen of them if you want. Just how special does it have to be?"

"Got any made of pure gold?" Joseph laughed.

Slowly Grace broke out in a glorious smile. She was so beautiful when she smiled with abandon like this.

"Maybe I do," she said, as if she had a secret or two of her own. She unbuttoned the top pearl buttons of her lace collar. She pushed her collar back and revealed a delicate gold box chain. She unfastened the clasp and without ceremony slid off two charms. She pulled Joseph's hand toward her and dropped the charms into his open palm. Tenderly, she closed his fingers around them and held her hand atop his.

"These belonged to my mother. She said it was a symbol of her and my father's hearts locked together for eternity. Tell me if this is what your Prayer Chest is missing?"

Joseph unclasped his fingers. In the palm of his hand lay a perfect, tiny lock with a miniature key laying beside it.

Both were made of pure gold.

CHAPTER 22

Three days later

When Mary was a baby, only her father's company would comfort her at bedtime. The nightly ritual was that Joseph would read her two stories, the same two stories. He could recite them both by heart. This is how it was with Malachi's three Secrets. Joseph reviewed the Third Secret as they packed up the belongings in the barn.

Prayer is answered when you welcome everything.

Joseph and his children joined forces to empty the house of its contents. Formerly cherished possessions were now no more than things to him.

Repeatedly fate swept into his life without apology. But like a cat with nine lives, Joseph kept coming back to life. What choice did he have?

Loss fertilizes the ground for gain.

Had the Mulches intended to be cruel? With so little time remaining before being forced off the farm, the Mulches no longer mattered. What mattered was the undeniable reality that Joseph no longer had the means to support his two children.

Welcome everything.

In the late afternoon Joseph sat at the kitchen table writing a letter, asking for a favor in print that he did not have the courage to ask for face-to-face.

"By spring," Joseph wrote in his best penmanship, "I will have certainly found a situation to allow me to provide for my children. It is an enormous favor I ask of you, taking custody of Daniel and Mary, this I know. But it is for them that I ask, not for myself. Forever in your debt I shall remain, Joseph Hutchinson."

He knew that this was too much to ask of Grace, but to whom else could he turn?

Although it seemed unrealistic that two opposite states of mind could coexist, Joseph wrote this heartbreaking letter to Grace while maintaining an optimism that was, thus far, clearly unfounded. Somehow the Prayer Chest had inspired a faith in Joseph that something might turn up in the next moment, something unexpected and wonderful even. Such is the mysterious power of faith: a belief in things yet unseen.

The evening meal that night was remarkable for its lightheartedness. They sat in the skeleton of what was once their front room, around a grouping of six crates posing as a dining table and three crates as chairs. It was the children's idea.

"Why not?" Joseph laughed. "Life's an adventure."

That he called it an adventure and not what it appeared to be, a tragedy, spoke volumes.

They were halfway through the meal, discussing the possibility of putting a second prayer into the Prayer Chest, when they heard a horse and carriage approaching the house. At six o'clock in the evening, unannounced, no one went visiting unless it was bad news. The Hutchinsons braced themselves. The three of them together opened the door to the Mulches.

Mixed feelings, all unspoken, abounded.

As head of the family, Joseph felt responsible to be polite and invite them into the front room. He made no excuse for giving his guests a crate each to sit on. Charlie and Daisy had made a fool of him once before; a lesser man might take his revenge, but Joseph would be satisfied with not letting it happen again.

He watched his unwelcome visitors take their seats, and he then noticed their downcast eyes and how Charlie looked as if he had slept in his suit of clothes overnight. They seemed sick at heart. Now it was pity Joseph felt, not fury.

"You must think us wicked people, Mr. Hutchinson," Daisy began, "and I cannot imagine what you felt Monday morning when our carriage did not call for you as promised." She did not wait for a response. "We did not come tonight so much to apologize as to explain. When you understand the circumstances that delayed us, you will realize that no apology is necessary.

"Going through town on the way to your farm that morning," she continued, "our carriage driver accidentally struck down a little nine-year-old girl. She was badly injured, and we took her to our home and have been at her bedside since. I spend the days with her, and Charlie the nights." Daisy's tears spilled down her cheeks. "The doctor said prayer is more powerful than medicine right now. But to be honest, it seems that's just his way of saying he thinks she will not recover."

Everything that comes to you is a portion of the answer to that prayer.

"Today is the first chance we've had to get out of the house so that we might let you know what happened."

Compassionately, Joseph asked, "What's her name?"

"Sarah," Charlie groaned. It was the first word he spoke since he entered their house.

Mary took Daisy's hand and squeezed it reassuringly. "Can we visit her, Mrs. Mulch?"

"I'm sure Sarah would like that," Daisy replied, managing a weak smile.

"She would," Charlie nodded. "Her parents died from the sickness a couple of years back. The aunt who cares for her has so little money, hardly enough for food, let alone a doctor, that Daisy insisted on taking her in and caring for her."

"Are you angry at the carriage driver?" Daniel asked.

"Jonah feels worse than we do, even though it wasn't his fault. Sarah was chasing a puppy that got out of her hands," Daisy explained. "She ran in front of the carriage without warning."

Compared to Sarah, Daniel's problems seemed small.

"It was an accident, but it could have been the death of her," Daisy added. "And knowing that we are responsible was almost the death of me."

"You have no idea how much my wife loves children. Every child she meets she treats as if they were her own." Charlie felt the need to elaborate.

"The doctor ordered us out of the house so we don't get sick from worry," Daisy added.

Passing through Joseph's mind like a nursery rhyme were the first words of the notebook.

Bring your prayers to the Prayer Chest, my son, and all that you ask shall be answered one by one.

"Of course, we have every intention of keeping our promise," Charlie said, "and paying you for this week's work."

But Joseph had not heard a word of this last sentence, for he retreated into the kitchen and returned holding the Prayer Chest in his hands.

"Oh. The chest," Charlie noted, a little uncertain.

It seemed to Joseph as if the Prayer Chest had a purpose greater than the Hutchinsons, one that was not meant to be kept secret at all.

"There is something special about this chest, isn't there?" Charlie asked.

Like a stone dropped into a still lake that causes ever-widening ripples, who could say how many families the Prayer Chest was meant to touch? Without pausing for preamble, Joseph shared, from the beginning, the story of the Prayer Chest and Malachi's secret writings in the notebook.

When Joseph finished Charlie said, "I must say I'm not sure what to make of it all."

All Daisy could think, however, was whether Joseph would permit her to use it for a personal prayer of her own.

Mary asked Daisy, "Where does she come

from? And does she have any friends? And where is her puppy dog now?"

Daisy knew the heart of a child. She answered the most important question first. "Her puppy's name is Otis, and he's sitting on the bed right beside her, loving her, licking her face, crying for her to get better. Oh, he loves her so, he won't leave her side to eat. We have to put his bowl of food up on the quilt."

Mary said she wished she could meet him. Joseph was firm about no animals in the house, but if she could only get him to meet Otis.

Daniel sneaked out of the room and returned with a gift for Mr. and Mrs. Mulch. "Here," he said, handing them each a piece of paper and the quill pen and ink, "write your prayer down. Poppa will let you put it in the Prayer Chest."

Written upon Charlie's heart all this week was a single prayer: *Heal Sarah*. Until the accident, they had had a different prayer, one they'd had for over a decade that had gone unanswered—for a child, a child of their own. But now their every thought was for Sarah.

The Hutchinsons sat in silence as the

Mulches wrote. Mary told them they could kiss the prayer before they put it in the chest; however, Daniel said it would not make the prayer be answered any better. Whatever Charlie's uncertainty about the Prayer Chest, he was sure of his prayer and so with little coaching from Daisy he picked up the pen to write.

Joseph paraphrased the three secrets for them as best as he could. He explained that the answers to prayers come through you, not to you. Joseph waited for this to sink in, for while it sounded simple enough, it was the opposite of what everyone believed about prayer. Then he explained that prayer is answered when you're listening to God, not when you're busy talking. Joseph hoped that the Mulches did not find this insulting. "The Third Secret is the hardest because the answer to your prayer isn't going to look like you pictured it. You've got to welcome what happens to you because everything that comes is part and parcel of the prayer's answer." Without Grandma Mary's wisdom or wording, but with his own plain elegance, Joseph conveyed the mysteries of answered prayer.

Charlie held the paper in his hand for a full

minute hoping to infuse it with all the desire of his heart before releasing it. Daisy did as Mary had suggested and kissed her prayer before slipping it into the wooden box.

Then, as if rejuvenated by the experience, Daisy took a deep breath, opened her purse, and laid six bills on the table in front of Joseph. "Your first week's pay. In advance."

If Joseph had been lost in the desert and just now offered his first drink of water, his gratitude would be no greater. It was more money than he had seen in a long, long time.

Charlie, the businessman, made Joseph an offer. "Let's say that as of today we have a one-year agreement, and you will do whatever carpentry work needs to be done."

Joseph shook Charlie's hand enthusiastically. It was more than an agreement, more than a promise—it was a lifeline. For Joseph and his family, it was a small fortune.

As if suddenly ashamed of spending this much time away from Sarah, Charlie stood up and said to Daisy, "We must get back."

"Wait," Mary said, racing upstairs to her bedroom. "Don't go yet."

She rummaged through her two tightly

packed crates until she found what she was looking for. Mary ran back down the steps to Daisy and handed her an unusually beautiful toy horse carved from a honey-colored wood.

"I call the horse Winnie," she said proudly. "She is my favorite."

"Believe it or not, Mary, I looked all through the house this week for a toy to give to Sarah, and I could not find a single one," Daisy confided. Years ago, she and Charlie had prepared a room especially for the day when they had a little girl of their own, but it was considered bad luck at the time to buy any children's toys until after the child arrived. "Thank you so much, Mary dear, and don't worry, we'll take good care of it," Daisy said, holding the toy to her bosom as she would a child.

"You better," Daniel said kindly, "because my Poppa made it." And with that he dashed out of the room and up the stairs. In short order, he returned with an armful of wooden toys. He dropped them on the floor in front of Mr. Mulch, and broke out into a smile as wide as the world.

"Oh, my," was all Charlie could say. He knelt down and investigated each one closely, marveling once again at Joseph's workmanship: a horse, a cow, a pig, a minia- ture barn, a carriage with wheels that turned.

Daniel's favorite toy was not in this pile. The dancing soldier was too precious to him. He was surprised that Mary could be so generous. It was a side of her he'd never seen.

"Joseph, could you make Sarah toys like this?" Charlie asked.

"Poppa doesn't need to make other ones," Daniel explained. "She can have these."

To which Mary added, "She needs all the love she can get."

CHAPTER 23

Later that night

🌱 Every evening, Charlie sat by Sarah's bedside as she moved in and out of wakefulness. He could not stop fretting about the utter poverty of her life. It was not just toys the girl lacked, but food, clothes, and adequate shelter; all the basics of life were beyond her reach. In talks with Sarah's guardian aunt, Miss Alva, he realized how brave a woman she was to accept guardianship of her niece while she had pitiful little money of her own. She made next to nothing, sweeping and dusting the shops in town after closing hours.

Charlie went back and forth, debating with himself how he might alleviate their suffering. Maybe the accident happened in order to bring Sarah and her aunt into his life? He invited Sarah's spinster aunt into his study for a frank discussion. Not one for small talk, Charlie said outright, "Miss Alva, what would you think about Daisy and me adopting Sarah?"

The offer rendered her speechless. Alva would have given Sarah everything if she could—but come winter there was hardly money enough for herself. Some bread and a potato sufficed for dinner on most nights; soups were created from practically nothing. Alva knew she was an unfit guardian, but at least Sarah *had* a guardian. How many orphaned children did she pass after dark, living on the streets? She made a vow that if she had but one coin left to divide, this fate would never befall her niece.

"Of course, you will need time to think it over," Charlie said. However, in reality he wanted to seal the deal this very instant.

Embarrassed to reveal her eagerness to accept his offer, Aunt Alva replied calmly, "I must consider what is best for Sarah." There was not a night when Alva was not consumed with anxiety about how much longer she could continue to care for Sarah.

Charlie mistook Alva's reticence for resistance, which instantly engaged the businessman in him. "After we adopt Sarah legally, I want you to feel free to come visit her any time you wish. And during the holidays, you can stay in the extra bedroom that we will soon be building. Stay as long as you want."

Alva, moved nearly to tears by his generous proposition, could not speak.

Charlie could see that his desire to separate her from her niece was tearing her apart. So he sweetened the offer further. "I might as well tell you now that Daisy and I plan to give you a handsome sum each year to help you meet your living expenses."

If truth be told, there were only enough coins left in Alva's purse to fit in the palm of one hand; this is how dangerously close to homelessness she and Sarah were.

Her silence tormented Charlie. He did not know what else to offer the woman so he stood his ground. "Upon one point," he added, "I am not negotiable. Sarah will take my name. She will be raised as my daughter. She will call me Father, and Daisy, Mother."

How could Alva speak, when to utter a word would open the floodgates of an unstoppable tide of tears. Tears of gratitude. Weariness. Relief.

The businessman was getting Charlie nowhere, so he took another tack: he lowered his guard and told her how he felt. "It would mean the world to us, Miss Alva," he said softly. "We do not expect to take the place of Sarah's parents, but you can rest assured that we will give her a life full of love and plenty so that she *and you* will lack for nothing."

She had to say something. "Mr. Mulch—"

"To be honest," he interjected, not ready to face her objections just yet, "it would be a blessing for my wife, Daisy, and a blessing for me, as well. More than you know."

"Mr. Mulch, you have no idea—"

"Don't feel pressured to make up your mind here and now. Take the night to think about it. Take the week, if you need."

"Mr. Mulch," she declared, moving toward him and placing her index finger to her lips. "Shush . . . I am trying to tell you that I accept your offer. As you can see, the only thing that I have to offer Sarah is the bloodline that connects us." Alva knew that this man was no fool—he could see her scuffed shoes and Sarah's threadbare clothes. Most men in his situation would have taken immediate advantage, but Mr. Mulch had treated her respectfully from the start. Like Daisy, Alva saw through the banker's bluff and bluster to the goodness of the man's heart.

"Sarah Mulch," Alva said, knowing how it

would please Mr. Mulch to hear it. "It sounds musical, doesn't it?"

"Sarah Mulch." Charlie spoke the words as if they were the opening line of a poem.

He said it again, but this time with a lilt in his voice. "Sarah Mulch, Sarah Mulch, Sarah Mulch." Together, they sang her name as if it were the lyrics of a song, over and over in different little tunes until they both tried but could not stop giggling.

Into this merriment Daisy entered, and for a brief second a wave of jealousy washed over her.

By the time Charlie finished explaining the turn of events, Daisy was in tears, hugging Aunt Alva and kissing her hands as if she were an angel come to earth.

Yet there remained the small matter of Sarah, whose condition had not improved. In fact, it had worsened since Monday when her small body was trampled.

The plans for her well-being were set in motion, but everything hinged on her getting well.

If the doctor was to be believed, she wouldn't.

CHAPTER 24

The following morning

Surprisingly, Charlie and Daisy returned to the Hutchinsons the next morning, and within minutes everyone was speaking at once. Daniel and Mary asked Daisy when they could meet Sarah. Mary asked Daisy if Otis would be there. Joseph asked Daisy if Sarah liked the toys that he had made. Daisy asked Joseph if Mary and Daniel could visit on Sunday.

"Tell me about the kind of toys you want me to make for Sarah." To Joseph this was the most pressing topic of them all.

"What do you think Sarah would like?" Charlie asked Joseph.

"Baby dolls," Mary cried out at their foolishness. "All little girls love their baby dolls. A dolly they can love and take care of on their own."

"Of course, Mary's right," Daisy agreed, inviting Mary to take a seat on her lap, "and

with the dollies come all the toys to keep
them company, like a baby carriage—"

"And a carriage with horses, and a doll-
house to live in with little rooms she can
sleep in and eat in," Mary announced, as if
presenting her own personal wish list.

Daniel left. Anything had to be better than
this.

". . . and little plates she can eat off of
and a little stove and beds just like a real
house but smaller."

Daisy tried to keep up with Mary's imagination but couldn't. She retrieved a book of
notepaper from her purse and made Mary
repeat her ideas, one by one. She made a
list for Joseph and when done, handed it to
him. "This is what I want you to make for
Sarah."

Then Charlie called Daniel back into the
room and asked him the kind of toys he
liked.

"Sarah's a girl. She won't like boy toys."

"You never know, Daniel. Some girls like
to play with toys meant for a boy. I don't
know her well enough to say, but, just in
case, why don't you tell me what you like."

"I like a slingshot and a pretend rifle, like
the one my poppa has for hunting. I like

blocks to build things with, too—lots of them, so I can build houses and bridges and even a whole town if I want."

Daisy wrote out Daniel's toy list on a separate sheet of paper for Joseph.

The two lists gave Charlie an idea. A big idea. Charlie Mulch did not become the bank president by thinking small. For now, he remained silent on the topic until he had worked it out in his own mind.

He left Joseph with instructions. "Begin with a doll, a baby carriage, a rifle, and enough blocks to build a town. That should keep Sarah busy." At the mention of her name he felt guilty that he was not with her. "Come, Daisy."

"May we send a carriage for you and the children on Sunday morning, Joseph?"

"Of course you can," Mary answered on his behalf, relieved that it was only two days away. "I can't wait to meet Otis . . . and Sarah."

The minute the door closed behind the Mulches, Daniel announced that they all had to write a new prayer right away.

"A second one? What on earth for?"

"My first prayer was answered yesterday, Poppa, and so was Mary's."

Without telling the children what his prayer was, Joseph agreed that, indeed, his prayer was answered, too. "But why do we have to write another one?" he asked.

"Why not?" Daniel said.

"Yeah," Mary chimed in, "it's good for the Prayer Chest to keep answering prayers."

"Poppa, have you run out of things that you want?" Daniel laughed.

"Nobody runs out of things they want when they know they can have them," Mary answered in her father's stead.

It was decided then. They all took seats at the kitchen table with their little slips of paper.

All the toys the children displayed to the Mulches were toys Joseph made for them when they were just babies. Joseph stopped making toys for them a long time ago. Momma explained that Poppa worked so hard he didn't have time to make them anymore. But new toys would be so special it made them giddy just thinking about it.

Daniel's fingers itched to write his single four-letter-word prayer: "Toys."

Mary's prayer took two words to ask for the same thing: "More toys."

Joseph was unable to write. What was there to want beyond his children's welfare? He honestly did not know. "I'm going to have to sleep on it," he admitted.

"You don't even have one thing you want to ask for, Poppa?"

"It's not that easy, Mary. Remember what Malachi said? Whatever you pray for has to come *through* you before it can come to you."

Mary agreed, even though she had no idea how toys were going to come through her. But she'd agree to anything if it meant she could slip another prayer into the pretty chest.

CHAPTER 25

The next day

Joseph awoke early. He bundled himself up in extra layers of clothing and quietly exited the farmhouse to brave the single digit temperature in his barn. No matter. It would be worth the look on Grace's face when she saw what Joseph had made for her.

By midafternoon he reentered the farmhouse. "We're going to pay a visit to the Browns," he announced to the children, holding up a burlap sack tied at the top with a piece of old rope. "I need you ready to go in twenty minutes."

They pleaded with him to reveal the contents of the bag and, of course, he didn't. "You well know that between the two of you, you cannot keep one secret. You'll find out when Mrs. Brown does. Go upstairs quickly and get into your good clothes."

The good clothes had to be dug out from crates, which only that morning they had begun to unpack. Every article of clothing Daniel and Mary retrieved was wrinkled beyond recognition. When they presented themselves to Joseph, all he could say was, "Well, you're clean."

They walked to Grace's farm, calling out the names of the trees that they passed, a game Joseph invented to take the children's minds off the cold. They counted forty-six trees. Before there were farms, or settlers to create the farms, there was forest; what was now forty-six trees might have been thousands.

Soon they were knocking on Grace's door, and she was inviting them in. Joseph wondered how it was that she always seemed to have a fresh fire crackling in her stove and a fresh bread baking when they arrived.

Rose danced around the room with Daniel and Mary in exhilaration at their wonderfully unexpected presence. Grace felt similarly, but in the place of dancing, she put water on to boil and laid out freshly churned butter and cornbread muffins.

When everyone finally sat down at the table, Joseph pulled out the mystery sack from beneath his chair and handed it to Grace.

"What is this, Joe?" she asked, eagerly

taking the burlap sack from him. "Parsnips? Potatoes? Old shoes?"

"Wait and see," he teased.

"Don't feel bad, Mrs. Brown," Mary sympathized. "Poppa always says that."

Rose made a grab for the big sack, crying out pitifully, "Please." Rather than have a scene with her strong-willed daughter, Grace handed it over. Rose wrestled the sack to the ground, trying to force open the complex knot.

"Rose, Poppa made the knot, so he can unmake it."

"No, no, no." She turned down all offers of assistance. Accepting help was tantamount to admitting defeat. Rose struggled on in silence.

By now Daniel would have ripped the sack open with his bare hands, and Mary would have gotten a knife and sliced it open. But they were guests in Rose's home, and they let Rose do it her way, even if it took all day. Even if it was killing them.

Thankfully, in time, the battered sack was opened, and a Prayer Chest similar to the Hutchinsons' was lifted out of it. Joseph took it from Rose's unsteady hands and handed it over to Grace. "For you and Rosie, so that all your prayers may be answered."

It was exactly the same size as Malachi's chest, in the same stained dark brown wood. Joseph had secured four elbow hinges from an old cupboard that he no longer used, shined them up and repurposed them for Grace's chest. The inside of the chest was bare wood, leaving Grace the option of lining it with silk or linen if she wished. The lining of Malachi's original chest was so moth-eaten with time Joseph could not imagine what it had been lined with once upon a time.

Grace held the chest to her bosom. She had never received a gift as precious. She searched for words but could only come up with, "Thank you, Joe."

"You're welcome, but you have to promise that you won't ask for your lock back!" Joseph smiled.

Overcome by emotion, Grace retreated to the kitchen, where she could express the fullness of her feelings by feeding him.

Each child took turns playing with the box until it finally made its way back to Grace.

After they had eaten and Joseph and Grace had covered the list of current events,

Daniel and Mary told Rose about all the toys Poppa was making for Sarah.

Joseph began describing in detail the kind of toys that Charlie asked him to create.

"Hold that thought, Joe," Grace said, hurriedly retreating to the kitchen, returning with paper and a beautiful quill pen in hand.

"Now," she said, "tell me what Mr. Mulch asked for, and then tell me how you see it looking."

As Joseph described the different toys he planned to create, she began sketching her own design ideas.

While Joseph's dolls were functional, Grace's were fully realized, practically life-like. He had the talent to create the outline of them, but not the ability to fill in the dozens of important details that breathed life into them. The way Grace sketched them, the dolls were more like babies than wood toys. So much so that Mary asked to take the sketches home and play with them. Joseph explained that he would make her a doll just like Grace's sketch, "if you want it."

"*If I want it?*" Mary stared at him. This man could not possibly be her father. Her real father would know that she would want this dolly more than anything without having to even ask her.

Grace winked at Mary and smiled, then turned to Joseph. "This is not to say your dolls aren't wonderful, Joe."

"Don't spare my feelings. I know what I can do. I just never knew what you could do until now."

They worked for nearly two hours without a break. Joseph and the children were mesmerized. Grace handed over sketch after sketch of a doll, a baby carriage, a horse-drawn coach, and a woodland cottage.

"Here, take them. Use them. They're yours," she offered the little stack of drawings as her gift to Joseph.

"Not without giving you credit."

"I don't need the credit."

"Yes, I forgot. Grace Brown doesn't need anything from anyone," he said with a mild sarcasm. "She can do life all by herself."

Is this how he saw her? She saw the tendency in Rose but not in herself.

He stuffed her sketches into his shirt pocket and announced roughly that it was time to leave.

The children were already on the porch when he turned back with a whisper to ask her a private question he'd been harboring all afternoon.

"Sunday night, after I return from the Mulches, I'd like to come by and take you out for a walk. Just the two of us." It did not come out sounding like a question as he had intended.

Grace flushed. She did not want to hurt his feelings. She chose her words carefully. "I'm sorry, Joe, I have an engagement." She left it at that.

"With who?" Joe said presumptuously.

"With—" she hesitated. It was not really any of his business. She searched his face, but not unlike his heart, it revealed little of what he felt. So, kindly, but without apology, she answered, "With Doctor McKnight."

"Rose's doctor? The one who couldn't help Rose? The one who couldn't save Miriam?" His temper erupted. He shut the door.

Grace met his temper with a bit of her own. She responded defiantly, "Yes, Rose's doctor." Since when did she have to explain herself to anyone?

He had no right; she did not belong to him, but he blurted it out anyway, "He's not any good, Grace."

"He's just a doctor, Joe, not a god." Was

this about the doctor, or Miriam, or something else?

Joseph had seen plenty of the doctor when Miriam was sick, practically every other day for three weeks. He did not want to remember how young and good-looking the man was; or that he was city-bred and trained, giving him a charm and polish that was no match for a farm boy; or that he came from a wealthy family. That this doctor was the perfect suitor made Joseph want to bruise her with his words: "He's too damn young for you, Grace. What are you thinking?"

A less-confident woman would have taken that reference to their seven-year age difference as an insult, but Grace deflected the blow. "Then you had better warn him about the danger of consorting with an older woman."

"I won't allow it," Joseph commanded, as if he were speaking to his daughter, not his friend.

"You forget yourself, Joseph," she said sharply. "What I do or don't do is not for you to say." She had no desire to hurt him, but she was not certain he felt the same. "I've been living my life just fine without you, Joseph Hutchinson."

He was at the mercy of feelings he could neither name nor control. "You're wrong to go out with him, Grace."

"According to whom?"

"According to me. And that should be enough."

"It would be if I were your child." Color flooded her cheeks and neck. "You can't tell me what to do."

"Yes I can. I know I'm not your father but I am your—" At this he stopped short: what was he to her?

"My what?" A sly smile slowly formed on the edges of her lips. "What are you, Joe? I'll tell you what. You're my friend. That is all you are because that is all you *want* to be!"

He was outraged—she was right. He turned and stormed out her front door, slamming it behind him to make his point perfectly clear—whatever that was.

Grace's temper turned to giggles. Soon the giggles turned to peals of laughter that she could not stop, until eventually Rose came out from her room, asking what was so funny.

"Men. Men are so funny."

CHAPTER 26

Sunday

Sarah was nothing like Daniel and Mary had expected. Late Sunday morning, when they tiptoed into her bedroom, she spoke to them like long-lost friends. She was talkative, affectionate, and interested in what they found interesting. Sarah was sitting up in bed playing with Winnie and sharing stories about her life.

Sarah occupied the pink bedroom that Daisy and Charlie had long ago prepared for the day when they had a baby girl of their own. It was fit for a princess. The centerpiece was the four-poster canopy bed draped on all sides with cream-colored chiffon. The bed had a half dozen oversized pillows resting upon it. The large windows overlooked a colorful wildflower garden and a pond. In a corner of the room was a bookshelf with children's tales beside a table with four child-sized chairs, the backs of each carved in the shape of an animal. Bright, airy, and colorful, the room would be any little girl's dream come true.

They sat together on Sarah's luxurious bed, swapping stories for the better part of the afternoon. While Mary liked Sarah just fine, it was Otis with whom she had fallen in love. Since first laying eyes on the furry pup, she swept him up in her arms like a baby, never once releasing him from her embrace. Mary's third prayer was all but written.

Daniel, on the other hand, was entranced by the raven-haired girl. Sarah was exotic, with her smooth olive-colored skin, dark almond-shaped eyes, and a hint of a foreign accent. She was one year older than Daniel, but much more serious.

Daniel had never met anyone like her before.

Looking different, she explained, meant that her family was treated like outsiders.

"People think different is dangerous."

"You don't seem dangerous to me." Daniel smiled.

"I am glad to hear it." Sarah smiled back, for secretly she hoped he would be her first real friend. She had not had a friend for the last two years since she began living with

Aunt Alva. Sarah would never say a bad word about Aunt Alva, her only living relative; however, these last two years with her were like living beneath a black cloud of worry—the next coin, the next job, the next meal. Sarah could live with a pocket empty of coins, but a life without play and friends proved almost unbearable for her.

Daniel asked her why she lived with her aunt and not her mother and father.

"When Mama and Papa caught the fever, Aunt Alva came to get me."

Daniel could see her lips quivering so he turned away. He thought of his two uncles whom he never met. They died of the fever but his father never spoke of them.

A little while later he said, "Alva is a funny name."

"Not if you are Spanish. It's a common name there. . . . Can I tell you a secret, Daniel?"

Since the Prayer Chest, Daniel's life seemed to be filled with secrets. "Oh, yes."

"The best thing that ever happened to me was being hit by the carriage and being brought here. The Mulches are so nice. They treat me as if I were their own daughter."

Daniel had never been with anyone who spoke so openly about feelings.

Sarah shared some things but not everything. She did not share what Doctor McKnight knew about her accident. She did not tell him how much her left leg and arm ached beneath the wood and bandage splints. She didn't mention about how the right side of her head hurt so much when she woke up in the morning that it made her dizzy.

"If I stay here," she asked Daniel boldly, "will you come visit?"

"Will I ever!"

Mary chimed in how badly she wanted to come, too, hoping that every visit would include Otis.

"Thanks for sharing Winnie with me," Sarah said, turning her attention to Mary, "before you even knew if you liked me."

"That's okay," Mary fibbed. "I have a lot of toys."

Sarah laughed at the differences in their lives. To her, holding a toy in her arms for even an afternoon was an extravagance. Aunt Alva used to say that toys distracted a person from what was important in life: work and money. When Sarah made the mistake of asking for a skipping rope she learned Aunt Alva's answer for every question. "Work and money are like air and water, young lady. That's what I'd pay more attention to if I were you."

With Winnie wrapped in her arms, she asked Daniel and Mary frankly, "Do you ever feel bad for children who don't have any toys to play with?"

Mary admitted that she had never given it a thought. It went without saying that Daniel hadn't.

"And yet you have both been so good to me," she smiled, apparently having given it a good deal of thought.

As if in answer to her question, the bedroom door swung open and in walked Charlie and Joseph. The anvil of dread about Sarah's condition still weighed Charlie down, but he had gotten better about hiding it. "How is everything?" he said jovially.

"It's good for us, Uncle Charlie," Sarah said, calling him *uncle* as he suggested, "but not so good for other children."

"What other children?" he asked, finding a spare corner of the mattress to sit down upon.

"I'm lucky. I have everything a girl could

want—friends, toys, you, and Aunt Daisy. But what about children who don't? What will happen to them?"

"You should be thinking about getting well, not the world of unfortunate children," he said admiringly. In his whole privileged life he had never given a thought to others less fortunate than himself. The feeling swept over him yet again that this accident was no accident. He eyed Sarah as if she were more angel than little girl. "What do you suggest we do about it, Sarah?" he asked.

"Daniel and Mary brought me these toys to play with, and Mr. Hutchinson is going to make me even more. What if I take one or two toys, and we give the rest to children who don't have any?"

"For Christmas," Mary chimed in.

"Well, it is funny that you mention this, little one. I have spent the better part of this day speaking with Mr. Hutchinson about selling toys to children. Why right at this moment we are planning to market and sell Joseph's toys. I have never seen an equal in craftsmanship, and if we price the toys right, I believe there will be a good profit to be made."

"I'm not talking about selling toys to children, Uncle. I'm talking about giving them away."

"Where's the profit in giving them away, Sarah?" He laughed aloud and looked around the room for confirmation, as if to say, had they ever heard an idea quite as absurd?

Joseph heard the love in Sarah's suggestion. He asked her softly, "What do you suggest we do?"

"My father came to me in a dream last night. In it, he showed me how Uncle Charlie opened the doors to the bank and there was a line of children waiting to come in."

Charlie realized she was not pulling his leg. He stopped laughing and listened.

"In the dream there were so many children who'd come, and no one was turned away. Everybody was welcome inside the bank to get warm, eat, drink, and be together."

Perhaps it was because she had always been treated like an outsider that Sarah wanted to offer a place where, even for one night, everyone belonged, everyone was welcome. "It was like a great big family."

"It's a beautiful dream, Sarah," Joseph said, visibly moved by her vision.

Charlie contemplated a way to make the idea work for the bank. Some cocoa and cookies will bring the bank a year's worth of goodwill, he thought.

"You'll need to give a toy to every child who walks into your bank, Uncle Charlie."

"A toy for each child who doesn't have a toy to call his own," Joseph echoed her sentiments. "What's childhood, Charlie, without toys?"

The businessman in Charlie was mentally objecting to a proposition that was growing increasingly costlier by the minute.

"Think of it, Charlie. We can use your idea to sell the toys for profit, but for every ten we sell, why don't we set the tenth aside for charity and give it to the orphans?"

Though less profitable, Joseph's idea was something Charlie thought he might be able to live with.

Sarah reminded them that Joseph's idea came from the Book of Malachi in the Old Testament.

Joseph and the children were startled at the mention of that name. They stared at her as if she had just sprouted wings. Was it the same Malachi?

"There's a Book of Malachi in the Bible?" Mary said incredulously.

She nodded her head. "Malachi says that out of every ten that you get from God, you give one back to God as a thank you. It is called a tithe."

"Don't worry, Uncle," Sarah reassured him, "you don't have to give away toys every Christmas. I bet if you do it this once, by next year other places will want to do it, too."

"How about we call it the Christmas Toy Bank?" Charlie suggested, delighted with his contribution.

That's when the room erupted in conversation. Everyone was laughing and making suggestions and giving advice at once, which caught Daisy's and Aunt Alva's attention and drew them into Sarah's bedroom, now a commotion of creativity and cross talk.

"I can't promise," Charlie said. "But I will see what I can do."

Sarah enjoyed seeing her father's idea spark the imagination of everyone in the room. He had taught her that the purpose of life was to do good.

"If we do this," Joseph directed his instructions to his children, "it means that from now until Christmas, you'll do nothing but make toys for the Toy Bank."

"This entire plan hinges on you, Joseph," Charlie said.

"Well, if it hinges on me," Joseph pointed to his children, "then it hinges on both of you, because this means you'll have to work very hard!"

Your prayer is answered through you.

Daniel and Mary nodded in agreement.

"Well, then, Charlie, it seems that we are all in agreement, all except one important member of this group who's not here." Joseph wondered if Grace would be talking to him after the other day.

"Who is it?" Charlie inquired. "If it is money he wants, I can pay him more than what he is making now."

"It's not money, Charlie, it's. . . ."

"What is it?" Charlie pressed him.

"It's, um, personal," Joseph mumbled, embarrassed that he had behaved no better than a schoolboy in front of Grace.

"Then you better work it out, Joseph," Charlie, the businessman counseled. "The Toy Bank can't wait."

Joseph's face reddened.

Daisy, the peacekeeper, immediately volunteered to help Joseph in any way she could.

So did Sarah. "I want to work with you, too, Mr. Hutchinson."

Joseph knew that to a girl like Sarah, a project with a purpose was better than anything Doctor McKnight could prescribe. Doctor McKnight—his blood boiled at the mere thought of him.

"Sorry to disappoint you, Sarah, but I'm keeping you to myself," Charlie announced. "You're going to work with me, as Vice President of the Toy Bank. We need to make sure the whole idea works, not just the part about the toys."

"If we're starting now, Charlie, then you'd better look at these," Joseph said, reaching into his shirt pocket for Grace's sketches.

They were far more sophisticated than the toys Joseph had shown him the other night. Charlie was impressed. He handed the drawings over to Sarah, saying, "I want you to choose which ones you like best.

And in the meantime, Daisy, give Joseph money so he can buy supplies. And get busy building toys."

Daisy marveled at the confidence and authority that Charlie exuded. At times like these she found herself falling in love with him all over again.

CHAPTER 27

Four days later

🌿 The Prayer Chest was supposed to be a rope let down from heaven but it wasn't doing much good for Sarah. Instead of improving with each new day, just the opposite happened and her complexion grew paler, her body wearier.

"If she wore her injuries on the outside," Doctor McKnight said, "like she did her bruises, medicine could better help her." What he was really saying was that no amount of Charlie's money was going to make a difference.

And while Sarah's body might have been slowly weakening, Charlie could not deny that her sheer will and determination to live was gaining strength daily. He stood at her bedroom door watching her sleep. He did not question how it was possible that in such a short time he had come to love her as his own.

He took a seat in the overstuffed chair beside her bed and waited. Charlie Mulch
wasn't a spiritual man, but somehow since
meeting Sarah he had become a better man;
his world took on more color, more dimen-
sion, more depth. What good was a pile of
money if he could not share it? He closed his
eyes and imagined the faces of the little children as they walked into the bank and saw
all the toys, food, and love waiting for them.
He could not help but smile with delight.

The next day, minutes after the bank closed
for the day, Charlie called an urgent meeting
in his office to discuss Sarah's idea. The
staff was comprised of a dozen men, but
by-and-by each had furtively wiped away a
tear or two in the course of Charlie's pre-
sentation.

"Can I invite my children?"

"Can I donate money toward the Toy
Bank?"

"Can I bring new toys to distribute that
night, as well?"

Every question shared a single theme:
What can I do to help? There was no lack of
support. Everyone's heart was open.

Charlie attended to the minutest of details. Instead of hiring the local tavern, he hired the local widows in town to prepare the food. He brought in the young adults to re-design the stark bank into a land of colorful, homemade decorations, creating a magical atmosphere for children who long ago had reason to stop believing.

As youngsters could always be found loi-tering in the streets looking for trouble, Charlie hired some of them to play music in the band. What was a celebration without music?

"Any boy or girl who wants to make mu-sic on Christmas Eve will be paid. The bank will provide the instruments." Charlie told them to pass the word along. On the night of the Toy Bank, Charlie wanted the streets and alleyways empty of mischief, and the bank full of fun.

At the end of each workday, Charlie headed straight home like an arrow aimed at a bull's-eye. He walked through the front door and made his way toward the pink bedroom where he was certain to find his beloved wife and precious Sarah. Without removing his hat or overcoat, he took a seat on a corner of Sarah's bed and the three of them talked of nothing but the Toy Bank.

In the late night hours, he and Daisy attended to the logistics.

"Tomorrow," Daisy explained, "I plan to pay a visit to Mrs. Brown to be sure that she and Rose will be joining us this Sunday afternoon."

"The more, the merrier," he laughed. Since Sarah entered Charlie's life he had become a very agreeable man. "What about Joseph?"

"I've already asked. He will be working nearly every day, but he would love for the children to spend time with Sarah."

"I'll have Jonah round everybody up. By the way, why don't you ask Grace if she'd like to give out the toys on Christmas Eve."

"What's the matter with you, Husband? Sarah's been counting on that job," Daisy reminded him.

"But if she's not up to it . . ."

"Oh, mother's intuition tells me that she'll be more than up to it. It's all she talks about!"

"Then we'll have Aunt Alva there to help her." Charlie made a note of it, for there were far too many things in preparation for the Toy Bank to remember them all by heart.

"I've arranged to send two carriages to the Hutchinson farm on Christmas Eve," Daisy proposed. "We'll use one carriage to transport the toys and the other for Grace, Joseph, and the children. I am sure they will enjoy making the trip together."

Charlie was not so sure, for he had seen Joseph's demeanor darken when Grace's name was mentioned.

CHAPTER 28

First of December

🌿 It had been more than two weeks since the children were allowed into the barn. The first thing they noticed was the brand new wooden sign hanging over the entrance.

"What's it say, Daniel?"

"The Hutchinson Family Workshop."

"This is *our* workshop?" Mary asked.

"Yes, this is where we're going to be working for the next month," Joseph replied proudly.

He took their hands and led them through the double doors.

"Oh, Poppa," Mary exhaled with a mouth in the shape of a perfect circle. The barn was the size of the moon: where once there were dozens of small stalls in which to hide and seek, now the barn was one big wide-open space. The shop area was filled with dozens of shelves and different-sized bins lining the walls, and long worktables, each one dedicated to a different stage of toy production.

"What happened to Eleanor and Moo-Moo, Poppa?" Mary asked with great concern.

Joseph led her to the far corner of the barn that was devoted to the animals and showed her that while their stalls were moved, they still had plenty of room.

He lifted Mary into his arms. "You know what I think? I think the animals will be really happy that we're here with them," Joseph grinned.

This made Mary feel much better.

Joseph spent the rest of the day showing the children what they would be doing for the next month.

Later that night, alone in their bedroom, Mary complained about the cold to Daniel.

He was unsympathetic. "Mary, don't you see that our prayers were answered?"

All Mary could think about was the toys she'd asked for and the cold. Daniel's response was not what she wanted to hear, and her silence told him so.

By seven o'clock on the following morning, they were already at work.

Joseph was impossibly happy this morning—his beautiful children nearby, a pocket full of money, and the freedom to do what he loved most in the world.

"Daniel, I'm off with Eleanor, and I'm leaving you in charge."

When Joseph returned four hours later, Eleanor was dragging a flatbed filled with pine and maple, each piece with a particular destination—as a toy for a girl or a boy, a cottage or building blocks, a carriage, a gun, or a game.

When the wood was unloaded into the driest corner of the workshop, Mary and Daniel were assigned their duties. Joseph taught them how to paint faces and simple clothing onto the wood with as much color and reality as their imaginations allowed. The work was divided this way, with Joseph building the toys and the children bringing them to life.

The Hutchinsons worked all day, day after day. Most evenings after the children went

to bed, Joseph would return to the workshop.

"Won't we ever get a break, Poppa?" Mary
cried.

"We have breaks for meals everyday,"
Joseph reminded her.

"But we have to eat our meals in the
workshop, and all we talk about is toys,"
Mary whined again.

"Remember, Mary, we asked for toys and
the Prayer Chest answered our prayers.
Now we talk about toys, think about toys,
and make toys all day long! What could be
better than that?"

"Playing with them!"

"I'm sorry we have to work so hard,
sweethearts," Joseph said to them, "but do
you know how important what we are doing
is?"

"Sure I do. We are making toys," Mary
said coldly.

"It's more than that," Daniel shot back.
"The Prayer Chest answered our prayers,
and now we have the chance to answer
someone else's. We have more, so we give

to those children who have less. Is that it, Poppa?" Daniel asked.

Joseph was impressed. "That's right," he answered, but his mind was elsewhere . . . three miles to the west to be exact.

Every afternoon, rain or shine, Joseph enacted the same ritual. He put on his overcoat and told his children that he had business to attend to and that he would return shortly. He closed the door of the workshop behind him, and, with a steely intention, began the walk across the frozen fields toward Grace's farm to explain himself to her.

With each step closer his resolve dissolved. Each day within feet of reaching her front door he turned back at the thought of seeing her and telling her how he felt. Telling her how he felt about *what*? That he was a thief of memories? Nightly Joseph hoarded images of Miriam like a miser his gold—moments spent with Miriam, conversations they'd had and laughter shared.

He did not know himself what he wanted from Grace as he headed out toward her farm everyday. She could not give him what he really wanted: a future with a guarantee, a rose without thorns, a life without death. No one could give Joseph that.

CHAPTER 29

*Christmas Eve day,
late morning*

On this particular day, there were four suns shining—one in the sky and one in the hearts of each of the three Hutchinsons.

Before the carriage arrived to take the toys to the bank Joseph, Daniel, and Mary joyously surveyed their handiwork: sixty-three toys. These were not the basic toys that Joseph had created in the past. Grace's designs were far superior to his. The horses looked like horses, the carriages had doors that opened and wheels that turned on their axles. The painted eyes of the dolls looked back at you with love, and their arms looked as if they longed to embrace you.

Lovingly, they wrapped up each of the toys and carefully packed them inside the sturdy sacks. Toy by toy, every one of their prayers was being richly answered.

Daniel heard the carriages pull up in front

of the workshop before he saw them. He raced to the door and poked his head out. "There are two of them," he shouted.

A feeling of immense satisfaction passed between Joseph and his children. Over the years they had worked hard on the farm— very hard—but never like they had this month, with such single-minded determination. Together, with the help of the two drivers, the five of them carefully loaded the sacks into the second carriage. They worked with a kind of reverence as if storing sacred artifacts into a holy ark. Not a word was uttered until the last sack was stowed securely in the open seat beside the driver. Then, at Joseph's bidding, they all returned to their rooms and changed into their best Sunday clothes.

In the meantime, Joseph made his way to the lead carriage and swung open the door.

"Grace!" he cried out as if bitten by a rattlesnake.

Sitting inside the darkened carriage, composed and serene, Grace Brown's demeanor was an open invitation.

"I didn't expect you'd be here," Joseph stammered clumsily.

"Neither did I," Grace smiled, "but Daisy

insisted that Rose and I travel with her driver."

Only at the mention of Rose did he notice her napping on Grace's lap. Joseph lowered his voice an octave. "It's not to say that I'm not glad you're here. . . ."

"It's good to see you, too, Joseph. I missed you." Everything about the way she looked at him spoke of a deeper meaning.

"Me, too," he admitted, wanting to say so much more.

Mercifully, his children arrived, and it provided him with a reason to tear his gaze away from Grace. He lifted Daniel and Mary into the carriage and took a seat beside them opposite Grace. The commotion awakened Rose, and now all the children were speaking at once.

He knocked on the roof of the carriage, signaling to the driver to move along, silently wishing that the children were not with them at this moment.

The carriage lurched forward, calling attention to their close proximity; their knees touched and even through the thick fabric of his trousers and her wool dress, they both welcomed the contact.

"What I meant to say," Joseph said stiffly,

sounding remarkably like one of his wooden toys, "is that I'm glad we're traveling to the bank together—"

"Joe? It's me, Grace! Remember?" This wasn't the first time she wanted to shake him to make him stop acting so foolishly.

He needed no shaking. He leaned forward and blurted out, "I have tried to see you everyday, Grace, but . . ."

"But what?" She dared not mention the occasions she'd seen him make the walk to her porch steps only to turn back at the last minute.

"Every afternoon I put on my coat and walked toward your farm."

She urged him on silently.

"I'd get as far as your porch steps some days, and a few times I made it as far as your front door. . . ."

"What made you turn back, Joe?"

"I don't know that it was any one thing." Sitting this close to her he could not imagine why he would ever want to be anywhere else but right here, with her.

Grace learned not to hurry him; Joseph would have to come to the truth in his own time.

How could he tell her that he was scared

of how she made him feel? So much more than he had ever felt with Miriam. "Grace," he leaned toward her and whispered, "you have no idea. . . ."

"What if I do? What if I feel it, too? Then there's nothing to hide."

Like a ghost, the image of the weak-chinned Doctor McKnight appeared before Joseph's eyes. He turned cold and looked away.

Grace felt his mood shift, but said nothing.

Looking out at the passing landscape, Joseph muttered, "It's not important."

"Joe, please, don't do this." If they were alone, she would have taken him in her arms and made him speak his heart. "Talk to me!"

Caught in an undertow of dark emotions, Joseph felt helpless to do anything other than retreat into the safety of silence.

Over the bumpy roads and in the midst of uncomfortable confinement and the incessant chattering of the three children, Joseph composed a prayer: *Please do not let the doctor be at the bank tonight.* He did not trust himself in that man's presence.

CHAPTER 30

Early afternoon

❦ When they arrived at the bank, the staff swung open the carriage doors and greeted Joseph and Grace like royalty: a king with his queen and their three royal heirs. It was a treat for the children.

A group of workers swept Grace in one direction and Joseph in another, and the sacks of toys in yet another; that was the last time Joseph saw Grace until the bank doors were reopened at five o'clock.

For the first time in its history, the bank was closed for business on a weekday: not a dollar changed hands nor a penny made in profit.

There was no way to prepare for the transformation that took place in the interior of the starkly furnished bank. Upon every wall and open surface was artwork drawn by children—figures of happy families and babies and farmhouses with smoke billowing out of the chimneys, and animals and rainbows and suns and stars covered every imaginable surface. Clouds of white fluffy cotton strung by invisible threads turned the ceiling into a perfect sky. The desks were concealed beneath the homemade quilts and coverlets. Everywhere you looked there was something colorful and sweet to eat. Chairs and benches were placed throughout the room, inviting the children to tell their stories, share their secrets, and confess their fears.

And Sarah sat in the center of the main room upon Charlie's chair, a huge brass-studded, burgundy leather affair, four times her size. In front of her was his colossal mahogany wood desk at about ten times her size, and on the wall behind her were shelves that Joseph had built to house all the toys. Except now there were more than sixty-three—it looked like there were at least double that amount from unexpected donations that had poured in throughout the month. Sarah was in charge of distributing each and every one of them—surely the most thrilling job of all.

No matter how much the doctor insisted on bed rest for her ailing body, Sarah insisted that working on the Toy Bank was the best medicine, and Charlie sided with Sarah. He'd seen how her dream had infused her days with purpose and magically replaced her pain with pleasure. While she could hardly walk unassisted, Sarah was determined to carry her weight tonight. Charlie agreed but with one proviso, that she sit on her throne like a queen bee in her hive, and let the worker bees do the heavy lifting. Sarah did not have the strength to object when Alva stepped in as her assistant.

"Don't you worry, Uncle Charlie, the love in this room is going to heal me by the end of this night," Sarah beamed.

Charlie prayed it would be so.

So did Alva. She stood proudly beside Sarah. Wearing an indigo blue dress, a gift from Charlie, she not only looked different, she felt different. Earlier in the day she had caught a reflection of herself in the looking glass and gasped with disbelief in response to what she saw. The sheen of her satin dress and the luster of her auburn hair, brushed one hundred times that morning, revealed a brand-new woman. Long ago Alva made peace with the fact that she was not pretty, yet today it was a pretty lady who looked back at her. With the crushing burden of financial worry permanently removed from her shoulders, Alva's inner beauty was free to emerge.

Grace and Rose had the table beside Sarah's. A sign was hung on the wall above them, "The Naming Station." This was the table that the children would go to after they received their toy, and they would have all the help they needed naming it. That was Rose's idea, she understood that a name practically determined the fate of the doll. It had taken many agonizing days for her to find the right name for Clarissa, her favorite.

The same was true for Grace when Rose was born. When Grace set eyes on her newborn baby's flaming red hair and heard her angry cries, she discovered her daughter's true nature. Once Grace named her, Rose could throw all the thorny temper tantrums she wanted, and Grace would always smile patiently. And as far as Grace was concerned, no other flower could equal the intoxicating scent and wild beauty of a rose.

Hearts were full of anticipation and bursting with excitement. But it was hard to say

whose hearts were fuller—those waiting inside the bank or those outside.

Between four-thirty and five o'clock, the
hands of the clock seemed to stand still.
Four fifty-five, fifty-six, fifty-seven, fifty-
eight, fifty-nine . . .

CHAPTER 31

Five o'clock, Christmas Eve

❦ Everyone had waited weeks for this moment to arrive. When the band played their first note, to the amazement of the children waiting in the cold, the two Goliath-sized doors slowly parted, giving the children their first glimpse of the miraculous kingdom within. The crowd gasped with delight, and a river of children began rushing into the bank.

Only fifty children were expected, but the crowd spanned the length of Main Street. The town used the Toy Bank to bring families back together: siblings separated when parents died; parents who, for financial reasons, had to release their children into the care of others; relatives who had lost touch with members of their family—came together.

In this moment heaven was revealed on earth. All prayers were answered.

Sarah's heart was filled with joy as she looked around the room at all the smiling faces.

Joseph walked over to her holding a plateful of treats. "These are for you, Sarah."

"Thank you, Mr. Hutchinson."

"No, thank you, Sarah, for your idea of the Christmas Toy Bank. And please call me Joseph!"

"I'll call you Joseph if you stop giving me the credit for the Christmas Toy Bank. It was Poppa's idea." Soon her adoption would become final. She would be legally the daughter of Charlie and Daisy Mulch. She would be Sarah Mulch. However, tonight she was still her father's daughter.

Tears spilled down Aunt Alva's cheeks. Let them fall, she thought, for tonight she was the most generous woman on earth. With great pride, she passed each toy to Sarah who was positively beaming. She had rarely seen Sarah smile in their two years of living together, but they were both smiling tonight. In her new dress and festive surroundings, it occurred to Alva that perhaps there *was* more to life than the hard, colorless existence she had known. Games, toys, laughter . . . all the joys of life were not luxuries, as she had all too often lectured Sarah; they were necessities. Only now did she see how wrong she had been. Life is more than just food and shelter, she realized, life is about living.

From across the room Charlie couldn't take his eyes off of Sarah, the answer to his prayer. As a banker, Charlie was expected to hold his feelings close to the vest, but not tonight. Not anymore. When the bank doors opened and the children rushed in, he was overcome. He had never known how much heartache existed in his small town. At his age, loss was expected; but here, standing before him, were so many children who'd already suffered more loss than he had ever known.

Charlie stood behind the second most popular table in the bank. It was covered with mountains of sweets: sugar cookies in the shapes of dogs and bunnies and cows and pigs. Apple, pumpkin, blackberry, and mince pies sat beside strings of taffy and bowls of red-and-white-striped peppermint balls. He poured each cup of cider and handed out each cookie to the children with reverence.

Later, like a mischievous boy, he took

Daisy in hand and sneaked back to the steel-reinforced room, called "The Fortress" for it securely housed all the important documents in the bank. A month ago Charlie would never have used the key to enter this room for nonbusiness purposes, but at this moment he was embracing his wife as if it were their wedding night.

Charlie smiled broadly. "Soon you will have to call me Father."

"Only if you call me Mother," Daisy grinned, counting the days until she and Charlie adopted Sarah. Her dream of becoming a mother had already come true. Daisy had spent the last six weeks mothering Sarah back to health. She'd refused to listen when the doctor had pronounced his dire diagnosis and she had offered up her own: Sarah was going to have a full recovery, be good as new, even better than before and that was that.

Daisy and Charlie stole one last embrace before trying to exit "The Fortress" unnoticed, but Joseph was in the hallway, waiting for them with a gift. "For you, my friend," Joseph said, handing the wooden chest to Charlie.

There were no words to express what Charlie felt.

With tears in her eyes, Daisy said, "You're a good man, Joseph Hutchinson. Your father would've been so very proud of you."

Joseph was taken aback. She couldn't have given him a gift worth more than those few, precious words.

With all their hard work behind them, Daniel and Mary were free to do whatever they pleased. This was their night. They danced to every tune the band played. They ate every treat they could stomach. They made friends with all the children and told them how their toys were made. They laughed until their sides ached. No one but Joseph knew how hard they had worked this past month.

The entire town was swept up in the celebration. Instead of spending this night in their small family circles, the townspeople opened their hearts to this much larger family. It wasn't until people began sharing what they had that they realized how rich they truly were.

There was so much happiness here, yet

Joseph could not fully enjoy it. He'd spent the night looking after everything and everyone, except Grace, whom he was obviously avoiding. He waited until Rose left with Daniel and Mary, before he tentatively approached the table.

"Well, Grace, you seem to be enjoying yourself."

"Everyone's enjoying themselves. . . . Aren't you?"

"No, Grace," he answered defensively. "I'm not."

She laughed. "Oh, Joe, how you twist yourself up over nothing. I'm right here," she said softly. "If you would just open your eyes, you would see that."

"I can't look at you without seeing *him*."

"Can't you let that go? It's a good thing that we're at 'The Naming Station.'" Pointing to the sign behind her table, she repeated, " *'The Naming Station.'* That's what Rose and I are doing this evening with the toys you built."

"What are you talking about?"

"Let me tell you, Mr. Hutchinson, exactly what I'm talking about. Allow me to give your behavior a name: Let's call it *'Jealousy.'* "

"You're . . . ," he stumbled. "You're wrong."

"Am I? What would you call it when at the mere mention of Doctor McKnight's name you run away? What would you call it when someone comes to your farm every afternoon and, instead of knocking on the door, turns away? What would you call that, Joseph?"

Yes, he'd been running. Who wouldn't run when the Angel of Death was chasing them? "Don't you understand what it means to be a Hutchinson man? Since the day I was born I've had a curse over my head."

Grace had had it. "How long are you going to use that curse as an excuse?"

His body tensed, his cheeks burned red. Barely controlling his temper, he leaned over the table pointing his finger in her face, and said through clenched teeth, "How. Dare. You."

The big bank clock struck the hour with seven resounding gongs, and Doctor McKnight appeared at the table right beside him.

"Is everything okay here, Grace?" Doctor McKnight asked protectively, motioning toward Joseph.

Without taking her eyes off of Joseph, she replied calmly, "Yes, Michael, everything's fine."

"Are you sure?"

"Yes. He was just in the middle of telling me something," Grace responded. "Mr. Hutchinson . . . you were saying?"

Joseph turned on his heel and weaved his way through the crowd toward the back of the bank and flung open the door. The cold air slapped him as he stepped down into the deserted dirt-packed alley. In a rage, he paced back and forth like a trapped animal. "How dare you say that to me?" he shouted at the bank door. "You have no idea what it's like to be a Hutchinson. . . . Nobody does! . . . And the fact that you're even talking to him right now, shows me you don't know the first thing about me. . . . After what he did to Miriam . . . my Miriam. . . .

"My Miriam! She's gone forever and I blame you, McKnight! I blame you, Rose. I blame this hateful curse! I blame that hateful farm! I blame every Hutchinson man who's died before me and left me here all alone! I blame you, Grace! But most of all," he growled, hitting his fist against his chest,

"I blame you, Joseph Hutchinson, for being such a *DAMN COWARD!*"

And there it was . . . the truth. Joseph collapsed to his knees and wept.

Everyone agreed that the Toy Bank was an immense success. No one wanted to leave; however, when the food ran out and the band stopped playing, people understood that the night had come to a close. Charlie was at the front door saying goodbye to every last guest. Grace and Alva were making themselves useful cleaning up. Rose and Mary were asleep in the corner. There were only four toys left. Sarah asked Daniel to take Winnie down off the shelf. Even though she had donated it to the Toy Bank, she confessed to Daniel how happy she was to have it back.

Although most everyone had already departed, the pure love that was shared in this room remained. Even Joseph could feel it when he reentered the bank.

CHAPTER 32

Four months later, Easter Day, 1807

Daniel speared the shovel into the moistened earth, digging a hole beneath the elm tree. He had to make a hole deep enough to bury their prized possession without fear that some animal would dig it up in the night. If he was crying, nobody would have noticed the tears amidst the sweat on his brow. On the other side of the tree was the whitewashed wood marker on the gravesite of his mother.

Standing in a loose, wide circle around Daniel was the Hutchinson family and their family of friends, all here to take part in the ceremony. Also present were Charlie's and Daisy's two newly adopted children, Nate and Hannah, brother and sister, whom they'd met the night of the Toy Bank.

"I don't have to tell you how the Prayer Chest saved my family's life this year, and you don't have to tell me how it saved yours."

Joseph did not like making speeches. "Now, Malachi never told us that we had to bury the key. All he said was that once we put a prayer into the chest, we had to let it go or it wouldn't work. Burying the key was Daniel's idea."

Daniel cleared his throat. "I think that burying it proves that we really trust the chest to answer our prayers in its own way." He removed the delicate, gold key from his pocket and looked at his father. Joseph nodded, as if to say, *Go ahead, son*. Daniel laid the key in the freshly dug ground.

Mary had something to add. "We love you, Momma, and we miss you, and don't worry," she promised, "we'll never forget you." Neither she nor Daniel would forget their mother as long as they lived.

Nor would Joseph ever forget his wife. How could he when she had meant the world to him? But the horizon beckoned, and these last four months had healed him of his past and freed him to live his life. So with an act as natural as the reddening of a maple leaf come the fall, and as inevitable, Joseph slipped his hand into Grace's.

Grace understood; she had always understood Joseph. She squeezed his hand in reply.

Charlie stepped into the circle beside Daniel. "If you'll permit me, young man, I would very much like to add something." From his jacket pocket, he pulled out Winnie, the toy pony. "Sarah loved this toy because of the spirit in which it was given. Your generosity, Mary, meant a great deal to her." Charlie's eyes welled up. Since meeting Sarah, he had learned to express his feelings, and since losing her, he'd stopped caring who noticed.

It was three days after Christmas when he and Daisy awoke to find that Sarah had passed away peacefully in her sleep with Otis faithfully by her side. The doctor had tried to prepare them for this moment, but no one is ever really prepared when the eternal sleep comes. They regretted only that they were not there to comfort her when the time came.

What the Mulches did not know, however, was that Sarah did not journey alone. At midnight she awoke to an image of her father standing at her bedside. He extended his hand and said that he had come to take her home, and that her life had truly been an open doorway through which so many prayers had been answered. She took his hand and said peacefully, "I'm ready, Poppa."

When the task was done, it was Joseph of all people who said, "It is time to move on."

The gathering of friends and family followed him into the farmhouse for the reading of the final pages of the notebook. They took seats around the kitchen table that strained to accommodate everyone. Joseph motioned for Grace to take a seat beside him, along with his two children. Mary refused the seat next to Grace and chose Grace's lap instead. Daniel would have done the same if everyone hadn't been watching. So he took a seat beside Alva which, in some strange way, made them both feel closer to Sarah. Rose had found her home on Joseph's lap; Nate and Hannah were happily enfolded in the arms of Charlie and Daisy.

When things quieted down, Joseph opened Malachi's notebook and read the final chapter.

I asked myself the question: What gift can a father give to his son that will last forever?

I once believed that providing you with shelter and clothing was enough, but I have since learned otherwise.

I spent this Easter day, dawn until dusk, recording the Three Secrets of the Prayer Chest so that I could give you this book of wisdom—a valuable currency, indeed. With it I have purchased a true faith, my son. May you do the same.

Joseph looked around a room filled with new relationships that did not exist a year ago and realized the truth of the Prayer Chest: his private prayers were not answered for him alone, but through him they were answered for everyone. He marveled at how Malachi's every word had come to pass.

Grandma Mary taught that repetition builds wisdom, and wisdom, power. To that end I ask that you join me each Easter to reread this book, and later with your children, and your children's children. Can you see it—the Hutchinsons as links in a golden chain that spans the distance from heaven to earth? Promise me you will, and I shall rest easy knowing that the secrets of the Prayer Chest will not end with you.

You do not have to know how the Prayer Chest works, you have only to let it.

End, 26 of March 1780

Joseph turned the page, but it was blank, and the same with the next one. He closed the notebook feeling incomplete, but said nothing. Perhaps he had grown too dependent upon Malachi's guidance and was not yet ready to let go.

Or perhaps there *was* something missing.

Later that evening the talk turned to business, toy business. Joseph and Charlie laid plans for the start-up production of three hundred toys for distribution to be available for sale by the following December. They had secured the name of their company months ago, "The Toy Bank."

Grace would be the artist and designer. Daisy and Aunt Alva would be responsible for contacting orphanages and charities in order to give them the tithe of toys produced each year.

By nine o'clock, Joseph's children were in bed, and the rest of the visitors were dividing themselves unevenly between the two carriages, with Aunt Alva and the children in one and the adults in the other. Grace finished rolling up her sketches and bound them with twine. She placed them into her bag and turned to leave, but found Joseph blocking her way.

"I don't want you to go," he said.

His frankness caught her delightfully off guard. "Oh, you don't? Well, then, what do you suggest?"

"Stay," he said, "just for a few minutes."

Grace could not help herself. She dropped her bag on the floor and extended her arms to him. "Come to me, then, and let me hold you before I go."

Joseph did as he was told. He entered the warmth of Grace's soft arms and laid his head upon her shoulder.

Grace shuddered as his lips brushed against her neck.

"They are waiting for you in the carriage, you know," he whispered, pressing his body towards hers.

"I know," she sighed.

"They will be wondering what you are doing, you know," he said, kissing her softly at the base of her throat.

"I know," she said, biting her lower lip.

"Don't you care?"

"No," she exhaled, "I don't. And neither do you."

"You're right," he laughed. "All I care about right now is holding you close." And without asking her permission, he kissed her on the lips. Hard. He knew it was wrong, but he could not help himself, could not wait another minute, not another second. His kiss could say what his words never could—how much she meant to him, had always meant to him.

And Grace felt the same.

He kissed her as if to engulf her, devour her even, but Grace was not afraid of his passion. She had known it was there all along, lurking beneath the surface. It was why Joseph pushed and pulled and fought with himself and with her these many months.

Joseph's hands began to search her out.

"No, Joe," she moaned and pulled back from him while she still had the strength. "I should go."

Joseph agreed, and then wrapped his arms more tightly around her waist. "I won't ever let you go again."

Only a single kiss was exchanged, yet in that kiss was a promise of what was to come when they married.

They lingered for a few dangerous moments with eyes searching, hands pressing, moving deeper into the swell of feelings. They wanted to but could not pull themselves apart. A need was rising between them, and their ability to resist was melting in its presence. The sound of a kiss was followed by another and then another, until there were different sounds, the sounds of pleasure from them both; the ache of having waited too long for this moment. Joseph's hands moved feverishly to the long line of pearl buttons that fastened Grace's collar, wanting to unbutton them, or tear them open.

Grace knew that it would go too far if she did not stop it, so she pulled back and whispered, "Enough . . . for now."

She was right. Joseph took a moment to compose himself, then lifted her bag and carried it to the carriage. "Good night," he said formally. But the eagerness in his voice belied those two simple words.

As he closed the carriage door, Grace met his eyes, and said with equal nonchalance, "Perhaps we will see each other again soon." What she hoped Joe heard was, "Come see me as soon as you can."

He stood watching the carriage leave, lost in thought. Only then did he notice that Grace's scent lingered. He closed his eyes and inhaled.

CHAPTER 33

Later that night

How in the world could he have forgotten? Joseph tumbled out of bed and stumbled in the dark up the steps to the attic with an inkpot in one hand and a quill in the other. Once inside the door, he lit a single candle, lifted the family Bible onto his lap, and turned the pages until he found the primitive rendering of a tree, the Hutchinson family tree.

"Forgive me, Miriam," he said, as he dipped the quill in the ink, tapped off the excess, and carefully wrote 13 July 1891. To some future generation these would be nothing more than words on a page, but to Joseph they were a part of his heart.

He was about to close the book but was filled with an inexplicable curiosity. His eyes traveled up the page, backwards in time, searching for Malachi's name. It was Malachi, who by teaching him the secrets of the Prayer Chest, had taught him the secrets of life itself.

There was Malachi's entry on one of the sturdier branches of the family tree: Malachi Hutchinson, died 27 of March 1780. That couldn't be right. Joseph rubbed his eyes. The light from the candle must be playing tricks on my eyes, he thought. He took a breath, looked down at the page again, and there was the date of Malachi's death in black ink, 27 of March 1780. Joseph's heart skipped a beat at the realization that Malachi wrote the Three Secrets of the Prayer Chest and died the very next day.

Epilogue, Easter 1939

🌿 On the first blank page of Malachi's notebook, carefully, legibly, Joseph had written:

I write this to you, my great-great-granddaughter, Clare Rose. One day, many years hence, you shall read this notebook and ask, "Who was Joseph to add his wisdom to the greater wisdom of Malachi?"

To which I reply: I am a simple man who was almost swallowed up by the sorrows of life were it not for the Prayer Chest you now hold in your hands.

For years Joseph had felt that there was a secret missing from the Prayer Chest, a secret which, if followed to the letter, would lessen the sufferings of life. Was there anyone more expert, anyone who knew more about suffering than a Hutchinson, for whom suffering had been a way of life?

Now one final blank page in Malachi's notebook remained, leaving little room for a mistake. With the utmost concentration, for at seventy-three his hands were no longer steady, Joseph wrote down the Fourth Secret of the Prayer Chest, a secret he had written and rewritten in his mind daily for the last many years of his life.

He reread the words, to be certain that they were honest and true, and then dated the entry.

Easter Day, April 9, 1939.

After waiting patiently for the ink to dry, he closed the notebook containing Malachi's legacy and now his own and slipped it into the top of the Prayer Chest. Joseph surveyed the small room, considering where to hide it. He continued what he believed to be the family tradition of hiding the truth so that it would be found when it was most needed. He wrote it for Clare Rose, the newborn in the family, but had no control over who would actually find it. It took him until sunrise to find the perfect hiding place for the chest.

He could not know that nearly seven decades from that night, his great-great-great-granddaughter, Kate, would stumble upon the chest in her darkest hour. He could not know that with Malachi's three secrets, the Prayer Chest would have saved dozens of lives. But with the Fourth Secret that Joseph had added, the chest would save thousands.

Acknowledgments

Our friend Brian Stark—who, like the Sage, gives and gives without condition

Our editor, Trace Murphy—who is every writer's dream

The team at Doubleday—who do everything with such excellence

Our agent, Stephanie Kip Rostan—who is wise in so many ways

My mother, K. Lorraine—a beautiful Wildflower who sees all of life as a great adventure

My beloved mother, Shirley—the most generous mother on earth

To Christina—my confidante and my first editor

To Doug—my brilliant friend

Especially to the leaders at Sacred Center New York, a spiritual community filled with passionate people who inspire us to no end